THE GRAYWOLF SHORT FICTION SERIES

Winner of 1985 Montana Arts Council First Book Award

FRIDAY NIGHT

AT SILVER STAR

STORIES BY

Patricia Henley

GRAYWOLF PRESS · SAINT PAUL

Grateful acknowledgement is due the editors of the following periodicals, in which some of these stories were first published: *Northwest Review*, *Cropdust*, *Cross-Canada Writers' Quarterly*, *Permafrost*, and *Plainswoman*.

Friday Night at Silver Star was the winning manuscript of the 1985 Montana Arts Council First Book Award. Funding for the publication was received, in part, from the Montana Arts Council, the National Endowment for the Arts, and the Jerome Foundation.

Cover illustration by Alexandra Boies.
The type in this book is Joanna, designed by Eric Gill.
Book design by Tree Swenson.

ISBN 0-915308-84-3
Library of Congress Catalog Card Number 85-82574

Published by Graywolf Press
Post Office Box 75006
Saint Paul, Minnesota 55175.

Table of Contents

FRIDAY NIGHT AT SILVER STAR

Let Me Call You Sweetheart

I WAS WEEDING the strawberry patch when Sunbow walked by the garden singing something bluesy in her whiskey-scoured voice. She was on her way to the loom-house.

"Hello, Virginia," she called. She squinted and did not seem to care that the sun had cut two indelible lines in the middle of her frown. Her graying black hair was twisted like a pastry into a knot. She wore a dress worthy of a summer day: a wrinkled silk she had found in the rag pile in town. The dress was printed with orange poppies and stained under the arms. I could see through it.

I sat back on my heels, glad for the reprieve from the lambsquarter and dandelions choking the berries. "Hello, Sunbow. When did you get back?"

"Late last night." She stepped into the shade of the nearest pine tree. "I'm going to visit Roger," she said. "Is he still mad at me?"

From the loomhouse came the wooden slap-slap of the beater as Roger worked on his current rug.

"He's worked the whole time since you left," I said. I knew this would assure her. Even though she had gone away and left him, she was still afraid he might take up with someone in her absence.

Her eyes smiled. "See you later, Ginny," she said, and picked her barefoot way among the basalt stones protruding from the path. I watched her go. She was a lovely woman.

Sunbow and I are the same age, forty-six. We have been neighbors for eight years and each year we celebrate the day she moved here and began building the A-frame next to the creek. We were friends right away, talking of our mothers and adolescence and betrayals, laughing as though these things had happened to others, had not left scars. We had similar scars, Sunbow and I. Around three years ago, the stream branched through the geography of our friendship: I chose to be celibate and Sunbow, well, Sunbow did not. Men are as necessary to her survival as water, or so she thinks.

I took off my chambray shirt, draped it over the splintered

fence post, and returned to the strawberries. I thought about dying and being buried in the mealy soil I dug in. The wooden slap from the loomhouse suddenly ceased.

SUNBOW'S DAUGHTER came to visit in July and Roger wanted to take her to bed. Christine is nineteen and ran away from the farm two years ago. She didn't go far, just to the nearest big city. She bought thirty dollars' worth of make-up and platform shoes and found a job painting sets for the Children's Theatre. Now she has a car, a battered red Volkswagen she calls *The Gypsy Moth*. She drives out once in awhile to let us know she is not like us. Christine is a well-formed child, but dyes her hair the color of rust or dried blood.

Crazy Heart built a sauna fire about dusk. Christine wore her underpants in the sauna and that is what started the trouble. The rest of us were naked and we are aging and showing our ages. Even Roger, who is only forty, is growing slightly thick in the waist. When Christine undressed we all watched since it is a natural thing to be drawn to that youthful beauty, the clean lines, the smooth belly. But she immodestly left her underpants on, giving her the air of someone special.

After sauna, around the fire, Crazy Heart made music on his dulcimer, and the fire gilded our bodies with flame. There was a gallon of cheap wine passed around and around. Sunbow stood up with her tambourine and shook it against her naked thigh and swayed to the music. I saw Roger begin to touch Christine's back, lightly, lightly, just fingers on her spine in the shadows. And I knew why he did it. I'd seen it so many times before: a situation ripe as a pear presents itself: candlelight or firelight, clean bodies warm with summer, music like a narcotic in the blood, heartbeats, bloodbeats, moonlight and wine, wine to wash you into touching.

Sunbow saw it, too, and she threw down the tambourine, pulled on a pale caftan, and stormed away into the night like a whirl of smoke. A tactical error. Without her there, Roger felt free to pursue Christine.

I left the fire shortly thereafter. I don't know what happened. Sunbow never told me and Christine hasn't been down since.

NEAR THE WINTER solstice Roger went away in his step-van to sell his rugs. He was heading south for warmer weather. He didn't invite Sunbow to go along. He told her he wanted to be alone. Before he left, Sunbow painted a small sign on the side of his step-van: *any woman who sleeps with this man will be cursed with perpetual menstrual flow.*

The days were short: we lit the lamps at four in the afternoon. Going to the outhouse after dark took on the proportions of an expedition. Snow fell for days on end. We were snowed in for a week and almost ran out of tobacco. Smoking was one of our pleasures.

Sunbow would come over in the afternoon and bring her work. She created earrings and other ornaments from feathers and stones and beads. She made them all winter and sold them in the spring. She sat at the kitchen table and worked while I made tea or poured home-brew and read to her aloud from books of poetry. When I read Gary Snyder's poem "To the Children," she said, "Raoul would have liked that." Raoul was her first husband, a mountain climber and vagabond. She licked the tip of white thread and held the needle's eye to the dying sunlight. "He believed in going light."

Poems and songs reminded her of the men in her life. No matter what turns and bends the conversation took, it always returned, like a lost river meandering in the same square mile, to Roger, to Roger's last letter, or finally and usually to Sunbow's problem, as she saw it, her inability to find and keep a mate.

At these times I listened. That was really all she asked. Her thoughts were like poison; spewing them into air dispelled their power for awhile.

IT WAS DURING this time, during the clean pure winter, that Crazy Heart came to visit in the evening. He lives in a dugout across the road. We had once been man and wife, lovers, friends. Seeing him sitting there, after so long an absence from my dwelling, I felt as though I was returning to the source of memory, so melded were our early years.

One night as a storm blew outside we drank hibiscus tea and he never budged to go home. At last I said, "Would you like to spend the night?"

He did.

It was good. We were under down quilts in lamplight and his body was the color of dried pine needles in autumn. We touched in all the old familiar places. Afterwards, he nested against my back as though it were habit.

ROGER RETURNED during the muddy season. Late one night I heard dogs barking and saw headlights and the white step-van grinding down the road in moonlight.

Sunbow came over early the next morning. Her face was swollen, her eyes red. Her sneakers were caked with mud and she didn't bother to tie them.

"What happened to you?" I said, pouring black coffee.

She sat at the table and held her head in her hands. I rolled a cigarette for each of us. A raw wind blew outside and I could hear the scrape of tin against wood from the cowbarn. The window behind Sunbow filled with huge putty clouds.

"He's back," she said. She tilted her head and lit the cigarette.

"I saw," I told her.

"He's got a girl with him, Ginny."

"I'm not surprised."

She took offense. "What do you mean?"

I shrugged and sipped my coffee.

"She can spin wool. She knows natural dyes. He wants to work with her."

I waited. The feather was missing from her left earring. She pulled a wadded handkerchief from inside her sweater sleeve and blew her nose.

"Well, it's not what you think, Ginny. He's not throwing me over. He wants us both."

"And?" I said.

"I don't know if I can handle it."

"Do you want to?"

At that moment Sunbow's face looked innocent as a young animal's. Her eyes were soft with idealism.

"It might work out," she said.

The school bus went by on the road and someone walked near the house rattling the milk pail and strainer.

I remembered a rainy night years ago when Sunbow had

first been my neighbor. Raoul – the first husband – had written from Guatemala promising if he ever returned he would play his trumpet at the crest of the ridge above her house. Months went by. That spring night the rain fell in black icy sheets. I was sitting in the rocker by the woodstove sorting vegetable seeds. I heard the song, the strained notes, and could hardly believe my ears. Someone, a mad man, was playing "Let Me Call You Sweetheart" on a horn far away. I put on my raincoat and went to the porch. There was no moon. Sunbow walked by my house swinging a kerosene lantern, deep in the mud. She wound around my house and up the canyon, over slippery scree and through manzanita brush.

After everything, she went to him.

The Birthing

ONE SHOT and the killing was over, quickly as trimming a thumbnail. Morgan walked away from the alfalfa field toward the dead goat. It was early evening and the sun had long ago loosened its hold on the canyon.

Angel came running from behind the house. She wore a loose white shirt and was barefooted and soil crept up her ankles like socks. Her braids flew behind her.

"Why the hell did you *do* that?" she said.

Morgan stood near the dead gray nanny goat and with one hand he absently thinned green apples from the dwarf tree. He held the .22 in the other hand, the barrel at an angle to the ground.

"Told her I would if she didn't keep her penned," he said. "Here. You take this back to the house." He handed her the rifle and lifted the goat in his arms and began walking toward the county road, toward the goat woman herself who had heard the shot and was waiting in the middle of the gravel road, but near her house, a quarter mile farther toward the lake. Morgan could see her waiting, arms akimbo, in a long skirt and a big picture hat. The pine woods behind her were blackening and the goat was still warm in his arms.

IT WAS their custom to hold meetings to resolve disputes among their kind. The authorities had never been called in. At the meeting Morgan showed no remorse. He had changed his shirt, wet his head under the garden hose, and slicked back his wavy blond hair. He sat nudging loose tobacco into the careful crease of a rolling paper, his feet propped on an applewood stool next to the cold woodstove.

Angel stood up first thing and defended him. "Morgan was forced to this. He didn't want to do it." She sat down then on the sagging sofa and pulled the nearest young child into her lap, murmuring to his neck and smoothing his forehead.

The schoolhouse was lit by kerosene lamps with soot-black globes and the light was a little skittish, like a feline creature among them.

Georgia, the goatherd, sat in an overstuffed chair surrounded by her four children. She tapped her boots on the linoleum floor and, head bent, stared at Morgan through slitted eyes. Theirs was a longstanding feud. When the little one named Banjo whimpered, she put him to the breast to quiet him.

After Angel spoke no one said anything for a long time. A coyote howled from the rimrock and two dogs wrangled on the schoolhouse porch, their growls low and menacing. At last a tall woman in an old band uniform jacket stood and spoke. "We've got to think about what we're trying to do. We can't be shooting one another's animals." Her hands were grimy with garden soil and she ran them through her frizzy red hair. "What do we believe in?" she asked.

Everyone started talking at once and no one was accorded attention. Morgan said nothing and Angel didn't look at him. She didn't like to think the father of her unborn child would kill a neighbor's goat just for eating apples.

"Hold it. JUST HOLD IT, PEOPLE," Sam hollered, his arms high, gesturing for their attention. The jabbering subsided, like air seeping out of a balloon.

Sam was respected, a leader, a hard worker, a strong wiry man people rarely challenged.

"I can't sit here all night listening to this," he said. "I've got chores. I'll wager most of you do, too." He wiped his face with a blue bandana. There were murmurs of assent.

"Okay," Sam said. "I'm going to ask Morgan to relinquish his .22 for three months. All we can do is let him know we disapprove." No one disputed him.

"What about the goats?" Morgan asked.

"And we will put pressure on Georgia to pen up the goats. I will help you build a pen," Sam said directly to the goatherd before she could say one word in defense of animals running free. She slumped in her chair, defeated. The lines were deep around her mouth and eyes.

"Meeting adjourned," Sam said. The people filed out of the schoolhouse, resuming conversations and laughing, drifting home in the cool night, quick to forget the conflict. Angel and Morgan were last. They stood on the porch and looked at the stars while the others dispersed. The cloying smell of the lilac bush was thick in the night air.

"Want to feel the baby moving, Morgan?" Angel said. She reached for his calloused hand.

"Sure, Sugar," Morgan answered, dutifully placing his hand on her abdomen. He kept it there until the baby kicked. Then he hugged her with the baby like a bundling board between them.

"Are you scared about the baby?" Morgan said.

"Scared?" Angel loved for Morgan to ask her how she was feeling. He didn't ask her often since they had quit courting and settled down to have a baby. She was nineteen. He was twenty-four. They had met a year ago at a healing gathering in British Columbia, linking hands in a circle of two hundred people dancing and not letting go.

"I mean scared of the delivery," he said.

"No," Angel said. "So many ladies have done it before me. It must be almost foolproof."

"Let's go home," Morgan said, and he took her hand to guide her in the shadows to the red house beside the rushing creek.

THE HOLY FOLKS came the first of July when the sun was relentless and the people sometimes gathered in the afternoon to soak in the deepest part of the creek, watching the water striders skim across the water and the nightshade curling around the cottonwood roots. They drove into the canyon in a rattletrap Ford stationwagon, circa 1956, blue and white beneath Arizona and California dust, and overloaded. The tailpipe scraped the first real bump the car came to off the blacktop and the tailpipe was lost, so that the holy folks made quite an entrance, a noisy entrance disturbing the quiet rising of the heat waves.

Morgan watched from the grove of aspens shielding the creek pool. They stopped by the mailbox and all three piled out of the car, two women and one man, dressed in graying, once-white clothing. Morgan stepped from the shade and waved them in his direction.

The three strangers walked abreast down the lane, kicking up small dust clouds. They stepped into the shade where they had seen Morgan. Morgan, Angel, and Sam soaked in the creek.

"Come on in here," Morgan said. He was sitting on a submerged log, thigh deep in the cool water, the lingering branches of a willow trailing around him. Angel's freckled breasts bobbed in the water like some lush riparian fruit.

The three strangers sat down beside the creek, but didn't get in. The women pulled their skirts above their knees and hung their legs over the bank so that their feet splashed in the water. The man sat a little away from them and took off his raggedy straw hat and fanned himself. He was young, younger than the women, perhaps Morgan's age, and slender and white-skinned, as if he ate too many vegetables and not enough meat. His shirt was open to the waist and a brass fish hung on a thin chain around his neck. His chest was hairless and white as wax. The faces of the women were lined and creased. Morgan reckoned they were in their thirties, though one seemed older than the other. They looked alike, slightly plump, with the same dull black hair in braids. There were rings of dirt around their necks and wrists, as though they hadn't been able to bathe in a long time.

"My name's Adam and this here is my family, these women," he said, and he gestured with an open palm toward the women, who lowered their eyes in a modest way. "Greta and Gail." He had a slur of an accent.

"Where'd you come from?" Morgan said. He was curious, but not wary. They were used to strangers passing through.

"We been on the road awhile. Started in east Texas. Tennessee before that," Adam said. "We're lookin' for a place to settle down for a bit."

Morgan and Sam exchanged glances and Sam shrugged and nodded his head. The milk cow mooed long and loud close to the barbed wire fence on the other side of the creek.

"We got a spot not far over there – across the road – where we allow folks to camp for a few days," Morgan offered. "It's right by the creek and off in the woods so you can have a little privacy."

"We'd appreciate it," Adam said.

"I'll take you over there if you like," Sam said.

"That's mighty friendly of you," the older woman said, her voice thick and sweet.

THE HOLY FOLKS set up a tipi before dark, a bright canvas structure like a temple in the juniper woods. That night they had a campfire and the people heard the rhythm of a tambourine and singing, a strange high wail and syllabic chanting in a language they could not decipher.

Angel went to visit them the next morning and took a pint of pickles as a gift. When she came home, Morgan was watering the rhubarb, wearing only cut-offs and sandals.

"How was it?" he said.

"How was what?" Angel said.

"The visitors," Morgan answered. He held his thumb over the end of the hose so the water sprayed and made a fine prism.

"They're okay. They deliver babies, Morgan." She knelt beside the first row of onions and pulled some pigweed.

"Deliver babies?"

"One of 'em's a midwife," Angel said.

"Do they all sleep together?" Morgan said.

"How should I know? They call one another 'brother' and 'sister'."

Morgan absorbed this information in silence.

"Morgan," Angel said, still squatting, "we're going to need a midwife soon."

"Maybe they came here for that reason," Morgan said.

Angel stood up satisfied and went into the house. "Maybe so," she said.

That night Angel baked a rhubarb-strawberry pie and presented it to Morgan. He insisted they whip the last bit of cream. The sun gave way to evening and they ate supper on the narrow deck of the red house. The cool air soothed them. Morgan talked enthusiastically about planting more fruit trees and maybe raising turkeys next year. Angel liked it when he talked about the future.

Nighthawks swooped and rose like rags on the grassy slope before the alfalfa field began. From away high on the canyon wall they heard the coyote cries of children at play. Angel felt the baby flutter inside her. An owl sang from the shadows and Angel held her breath and listened for the holy folks. They were so far away, a quarter mile at least, and she couldn't tell if she heard them or just imagined she heard them.

Morgan went into the house and returned with a sweater for each of them. "Here," he said, "it's chilly already."

Angel just draped the sweater around her shoulders.

"He's a man of the Lord, Morgan," she said.

"Who?"

"Adam. You know," Angel said.

"Oh yeah?"

"He talks about the Lord's will and the Lord's love all the time."

"Talk's cheap, Angel," Morgan said.

Angel seethed inside. "You don't believe in anything, Morgan Riley."

Morgan didn't respond and after a minute Angel went into the house. Morgan followed her and in the loft under the blanket he said, "I do believe in you and me and our land, Angel." He put his arms around her and cradled her head in his hand.

THE HOLY FOLKS stayed into August and became almost a part of the community. Greta and Gail offered to help with the barn repairs. They didn't seek out a winter

beside the left front wheel, since squatting and rising had become strenuous.

Morgan stuck his head out from under the truck. "Fixin' the brakes, 'case we have to take you to town," he said. His hands and bearded face were streaked with grease.

"Sure is a nice night tonight," Angel said. She sighed and looked toward the creek, keeping her hands folded on her belly. "I saw the heron that lives back there."

Morgan disappeared under the truck again. Angel heard the gravelly sound of him scooting in the dirt on his back. The sky and the horizon seemed to meld in a blue wash and she thought she saw the silhouette of a deer in the alfalfa field.

"Adam plays a silver flute, Morgan," she said.

"Is that right," Morgan said. His voice was faint, disinterested.

"He says he can heal the sky after rain with his flute."

"You got a package today, Angel," Morgan said. "From your mother."

Angel's eyes opened wide. "Where is it?"

"In the house by the radio. Sam brought it from town."

Angel walked to the house and Morgan worked on the brakes until dark.

IT WAS the end of August and the grass was brown as palominos. The people were beginning to journey into the fir woods to gather firewood. Each day Angel and the other women laid out sliced apricots and peaches and pears to dry in the sun. Against the coming barrenness they stored great glass jars full to the brim with the leathery fruit. Batches of wine were begun in clay crocks and the smell attracted insects to the sweet rot. Tomatoes were bending their mother stems and even melons ripened despite the short growing season. There was a sense of accomplishment among the people. They had worked the land and the land had yielded a good harvest. Weather had been with them.

Angel's water broke at high noon while she gathered small green eggs from her chickens. The wetness spilled down her left leg and she remembered wetting her pants as a child and feeling ashamed.

"Morgan. Morgan," she shouted from the fenced-in chicken yard. Morgan looked up from the black plastic pipe emerging from the shower tank he was repairing. The hens chattered around Angel and she waved like someone arriving home.

"My water broke," she said. Then she shooed the chickens and slipped through the gate and locked it.

Morgan met her on the path and put one arm around her shoulders.

"I feel a tightening down there," she said. She held one hand on the underside of her belly.

"Does it hurt?" Morgan said, squinting in the sun.

"No, it doesn't hurt," she said. "I'll take the eggs to the house. You go tell Greta."

"You want me to go to the house with you first?"

"No, I'm okay," Angel said. She lifted the egg basket and then said, "Morgan, I want to have it here. No hospital."

"We will, Angel," Morgan said and he walked down the path toward the county road. He didn't look back. His worn workshirt was the same color as the bachelor buttons bordering the path.

Angel carefully placed the eggs in a cardboard carton and set them in the cooler in the shade of the back porch. The creek curved behind the house, silver from the sun, gurgling incessantly in a comforting way. Rude Steller jays hawked at Angel and she knew a small sadness, an awareness that she would never be the same again, that time was passing, that something irrevocable was about to occur. She went in the house ravenously hungry and ate two banana muffins with butter. Then she sat rocking and rocking next to an open window with the pocket watch on the cedar chest beside her.

"I'm coming, Angel," Greta said, as she slammed the screen door.

"No hurry," Angel said.

Greta unloaded a woven shopping bag on the kitchen counter, then turned to Angel with her hands on her hips. She wore a pale shirtwaist that nearly trailed the floor. Her hair was braided and pinned like a helmet against her head. She was sunburned, the skin at her neck fleshy and wrinkled.

"Are you timing the contractions?" she asked.

"Uh-huh," Angel said. "They're not real regular yet."

"Well, keep timing. They'll most likely get regular as they get closer."

"Where's Morgan?" Angel said. She glanced out the open window.

"Checking something on the truck," Greta said. "Where are the sterile linens?"

"Up there," Angel said, and she nodded toward the high shelf of the pantry, above the canned peaches and cherries and pickles.

Greta reached high and brought down the brown grocery bag which Angel had stapled shut and baked in a slow oven. It contained two white sheets and several towels.

"What about the floss and scissors?" Greta asked.

"Right here on the cedar chest," Angel answered. "We got plenty of time." She smiled at Greta in a shy way, then lowered her eyes and folded and unfolded the hem of her smock. It barely reached her knees and she wore nothing underneath.

"Did you buy the shepherd's purse?" Greta said.

"Yes. It's in that little brown crock."

"I'll make a tea of it just in case we need it. Won't hurt to let it boil and boil. You'll need a strong brew if there's much bleeding." And Greta set to work building a fire in the cookstove.

The two rooms were joined by a step up and a double open doorway and Angel could see Greta as she bustled around the kitchen, crumpling newspaper for firestarter, poking around for kindling. It felt good to have someone there to build a fire, make tea, and keep her company. Angel gathered a bundle of yellow yarn from the floor and began crocheting, the shiny silver hook slipping in and out of the yarn like a cat. She was making a bootie the length of a matchstick.

After a while Morgan came in with an armload of split wood. He stacked the wood, then came and stood between the kitchen and the main room. Angel stopped rocking.

"How are you?" he said. He seemed far away.

"Okay. Twenty minutes apart," she said. "Maybe it's a false alarm."

"Do you think so?"

"No, not really, Morgan. This is it."

"Do you need me yet? I thought since Greta was here I could finish fixing the shower and maybe do some other chores."

"I guess I don't need you yet."

"Okay. Just holler, Greta, if she gets close," Morgan said, and he was gone, out the front door into the sun's glare. Angel watched him until he walked out of sight past the garden's tall corn stalks.

"He'll be back," Greta said from the kitchen. "You got a ways to go yet."

"I know," Angel said, and she commenced rocking again and was comforted by the rocker's squeak.

Greta made a cool hibiscus tea with raw honey and the two women sat suspended in the afternoon, in the shade of the main room, gossiping and sharing a secret now and then, a shard of the past. It might have been any lazy afternoon, two women drinking tea and talking, but for the pocket watch ticking away Angel's innocence. The contractions grew closer and more intense so that when one came Angel's speech was slow and distant and she would still be telling her story but it was as if another person spoke and she, Angel, had gone way inside, concentrating on the force certain as moontide, the force that would wash the child into the world.

When evening came and the nighthawks began their ritual swing across the yard, Angel had reached a plateau and her contractions grew no closer.

"I should fix Morgan's supper," she said.

"Don't you worry 'bout his supper," Greta said. "He'll eat somewhere, no doubt. Or I'll fix him something when he comes home."

"Where is he, I wonder?" Angel said.

"I'm home," Morgan shouted, a grin on his face. "Thought I'd never get through at Sam's. They fed me, then I felt obliged to help with the milking."

Angel met him at the door and hugged him hard.

"I'm glad you're here," she said. In the back of her throat her voice flinched in fear.

"I figured Greta would call if you needed me," he said.

"I would have," Greta said. She dealt herself a hand of solitaire on the kitchen table.

"Why, you haven't even made the bed yet," Morgan said. He had built a plywood platform for a single mattress because he didn't want her climbing the loft ladder.

"We don't do that until it's real close," Angel said. "To keep the sheets sterile." She held his large, stained hand as though it were an anchor in rough sea. The light around them dimmed and Angel danced into her next contraction.

Greta silently picked up the watch and noted the time.

"Does it hurt?" Morgan said.

"Yes. Yes, it hurts," Angel said. "But maybe that means it'll be over soon."

"Let me clean up a bit, Sugar. Then I'll sit with you," he said, and he untangled her hands from his arm.

Morgan went into the kitchen and Angel lit a lamp beside the single bed. She sat on the bed for a moment, but then moved to the rocker. She liked to think of rocking the baby to sleep in her arms. And she would sing.

Greta finished her cards and sat shuffling the deck.

"How long could this go on?" Angel asked.

"First babies generally take their time," Greta said. "We might as well settle in for the night."

The night was a long one. At first Morgan and Angel and Greta tried to play hearts, but Angel could not concentrate and Morgan's presence disturbed the intimacy the two women had earlier established, so the talk was dull and desultory. Morgan grew restless and often went to the porch to watch the stars in the sky. Angel sweated and her hair grew tangled and she was alternately subdued and fretful. Once when Morgan was outside fetching kindling – they had let the fire die out – he heard a sharp cry and he ran to the door, but only looked in and saw Angel was still in the rocker and the bed still unmade, so he returned to his task.

In the dark hour before dawn, Greta made the bed with the sterile sheets and Angel, spent and trying to breathe in the proper way, but often crying out, went into the bed and bathed herself with wheat germ oil to lessen the chance of tearing. Her contractions were two minutes apart. They waited and her screams reverberated around the small house, shaking the salvaged barn-board walls and Morgan's heart.

Roosters fiddled at the skywash and Venus pinned the pink shell above the canyon. It was a cool morning, portending autumn. Morgan had dozed fitfully, unable to stay awake during the last hour. Angel longed for sleep and release from the pain. And still the baby would not be born. Greta had held her hand all night and once said, "You've got the hands of a child." The words stuck in Angel's mind.

When the morning grew light enough to see, Greta stirred from Angel's side and blew out the lamp.

"Greta," Morgan said, "don't you think she needs a doctor?"

"Not yet," Greta answered. "It's just hard work, Morgan."

Angel looked as though she had worked hard, her eyes puffy, her face pale. She lay on the bed with her legs bent and apart, the sheet covering her like a tent. The tent was open at her feet and Greta reached under now and then and measured her dilation.

"Four fingers," Greta announced. "Morgan, she needs you now. You stay by her. I must go out for a moment." And she left the house in a hurry, her skirts switching.

"Morgan, it hurts so bad. I can't believe how much it hurts," Angel said. She spoke quickly, desperately.

Morgan took her hand but didn't answer. When her body clenched, she clenched his hand, but it was limp and his eyes avoided hers.

"I want Greta," Angel said.

"She'll be back."

"Morgan." She screamed his name. "Mor-GAN!" And her body tensed, her back and legs arching in the pain and she could not believe it hurt the way it did. She wished to die.

When Greta returned, she had Adam with her. He walked in as though he belonged there and he was fresh and clean in white pants and a white shirt. He was like a vision to Angel. He went to her side.

"You're having a hard time, Angel?"

"Yes, God, yes, it's awful," Angel said, and she cried.

"When did this labor begin?" Adam asked.

"Yesterday noon," Morgan said.

"We've got to help her have this baby. She's wearing herself down," Adam said.

"Listen, Adam, I want to take her to the hospital," Morgan said. His hands shook like aspen leaves.

"No. NO," Angel screamed.

"We can do it here," Adam said.

Then Morgan saw the other man's eyes lock with Angel's and his heart spoiled within, ripe with bitterness.

"Adam, I'm afraid," Angel said. She groped for his hand.

"There's nothing to be afraid of," Adam said. "Be strong."

"I said I'm taking her to town," Morgan blurted. He spread his feet in a defensive stance.

"She needs a coach, someone to help her through. It won't take long," Adam said. "I can do it."

Morgan felt as though he were invisible.

"Yes. Yes," Angel said, breathless and panting and up on her elbows. "Adam, stay with me."

Then she cried in longing, a cry so raw with want and need that Morgan turned away.

"Son-of-a-bitch," he whispered, beating his fist into his palm.

His face was flushed and contorted in anger. He slammed the door hard and rode the morning like a man in a foreign country, a man with no home, working to obliterate the sound of Angel screaming.

And even as she held the waxy child, so new, with sky and clouds in each pale eye, Angel could hear the dull thud of Morgan splitting sugar pine as he had split her.

Victory

MARY RUTH woke up as her father shuffled in his slippers down the linoleum hallway, down the stairs, to the front door. He was home from Vietnam and she was unaccustomed to his presence in the house. There was no privacy; her bedroom and her parents' bedroom were directly across the hall from one another. Her room had no door. Her parents' room had a curtain of off-white monk's cloth, gathered and held aside during the day with a macramé belt Mary Ruth had made in fifth grade.

The cat darted into her room and leaped upon the bed, meowing. Haines, her father, stood at the doorway, a dark stone in the liquid night.

"Don't come in here," Mary Ruth said. She hadn't slept well. She was waiting for the first real light, the blue bars of dawn on her floor, then she was planning to go to work, to escape. Mary Ruth was fourteen and worked in an orchard packing house, packing pears.

"I just let the cat in," Haines said.

"You make me sick," Mary Ruth said, each word a razor's cut.

THE FURNITURE in her room emerged from the darkness like gray building blocks. Mary Ruth slipped from the bed and in quick, silky movements dressed in jeans, a flannel shirt, and sneakers. She rummaged in a daypack for cigarettes and a hairbrush, then braided her blond hair in a loose, thick braid down her back. Over this she tied a paisley scarf. She looked in the mirror, satisfied.

Six steps to the end of the hallway and she was outdoors, breathing the sweet morning, and down the steps no one used but her. She liked to think it was her private entrance. Perhaps she lived in a boarding house where no one knew her, where she could come and go at all hours, drop out of school, take lovers, and drink sloe gin. She knew about life. She had worked in the packing house all summer, with older women. Listening, she had learned quite a bit, and now she felt she knew all there was to know *in the mind.*

Behind the house there was one row of apple trees, then

behind that, a waist-high stone fence, and beyond that, the river. She climbed on the fence and walked the stones for a mile. She knew the fence by heart, never tripping. The sky was lightening, with a few clouds tinged brassy bright. She walked by a neighbor's Jersey milk cow, licking a salt block with her pale tongue. The salt block pleased Mary Ruth. She walked by it nearly ever morning and noted its demise, the depression from the licking growing deeper every day. It reminded her of the worn floor boards at school under the drinking fountain.

The stone fence ended at the river highway. The sun splayed over the hills, spilling on the river, a metallic flow. She walked across the ugly green bridge, ignoring the cars and trucks inches away. On the town side of the bridge there was a store, La Tienda de Pobre, housed in a pink stucco building with a corrugated tin roof. The words, *Tortillas, Beer, Cigarettes,* were painted on the side of the store facing the bridge, so that anyone driving in from the country could see them a half-mile away. Mary Ruth went in for a cream soda.

La Tienda de Pobre was owned and operated by Maggie, a dark, fertile-looking woman, squat and round, with breasts like overripe squash and eyes that some called bedroom eyes, knowing one moment, innocent the next. She wore ropes and ropes of jewelry around her neck and arms. All summer she wore a silver bracelet high on her upper left arm, a snake coiled, its tiny forked tongue flicking. Maggie had a moustache of black down, like the softest baby hair.

She kept the store open from five in the morning until eleven at night. Inside there was a potbellied stove where the men gathered on apple crates to gossip in the fall and winter months. House plants flourished in plastic pots and rusted honey cans. There was an old pool table, with latticed leather pockets. Maggie charged a dime a game, no betting.

"A SODA is not a good breakfast for such a pretty girl," Maggie said.

"I'm not hungry," Mary Ruth said. She shoved a quarter across the counter. She went over to the woodstove and stood with her back to the morning fire, drinking the soda, her pack over one shoulder. A portable television was on in a corner behind the counter, rolling with the horizontal out of control, a man's authoritative voice recounting the news.

Maggie played solitaire on the counter. Her fingernails were long and painted the color of winesaps, her cuticles ragged. She flipped the cards with an indifference and patience Mary Ruth admired, as though she would play solitaire all her life and not mind. The fly-speckled Pepsi clock above the door read six forty-five.

"What time you have to be at work?" Maggie said.

"Seven," Mary Ruth answered.

"Come here. I'll tell your fortune."

"I don't need my fortune told," Mary Ruth said.

Maggie shrugged, her eyelids heavy, creased with shiny green eyeshadow. She gathered the cards, mechanically shuffling and splitting the deck. Mary Ruth lit a cigarette.

"I do not need the cards. I can read your fortune in the way you braid your hair," Maggie said. Mary Ruth puffed hard, holding the filterless cigarette between her thumb and forefinger. "Oh yeah?" She turned around, her back to Maggie, and removed the paisley scarf.

The television flickered, a greasy gray light in the room.

"There is misunderstanding in your life," Maggie said.

"Ha," Mary Ruth said, crushing the cigarette butt into a beanbag ashtray on the edge of the pool table. "Everyone is misunderstood."

Maggie turned to a sink and filled a watering can with tepid water. "Do not take it seriously," she shrugged. "Smoke cigarettes and drink cream soda."

Mary Ruth tied her scarf with a jerk. Her lips were drawn down at the corners and she felt a hot, sour feeling, a tightening in her throat. "I'm going. See you, Mags." She slipped to the door and slammed outside, rattling the loose panes of glass in the door.

One block from the store, she took a short cut down an alley which ran along a canal. The canal smelled fishy and styrofoam cups floated in its murky waters. A car crept up behind her. She knew without looking it was Franny in his '53 Chevy. He worked at the packing house, loading trucks. Only women sorted and packed.

"Hey, Sugar," he said, slowing to a crawl beside her, hanging out the window, one hand on the knob of the steering wheel. Mary Ruth knew that knob had a picture on it of a woman wearing a bit of gauzy curtain. She had examined it closely once when Franny went into the store for something. Now, with his hand on the knob, and his voice on her, she felt excited, but she ignored him. She didn't want to get into that car. Then it would be all over.

"Let me give you a ride to work," he said. His hair was slicked back, his face ruddy and scrubbed.

"I can walk," she said. "It's just two more blocks."

Two dogs, hound mongrels, knocked over a garbage can behind a brick building and growled over the contents.

Franny reached for Mary Ruth, but she had expected that and ducked away. He gunned the engine and splashed through the mud puddles, tooting his horn and watching her in the rearview mirror.

The rest of the way to work she thought of the smooth, lethal sound of the word *sugar* when Franny said it. Sometimes he came by and said, *gimme some sugar* and she thought she knew exactly what he meant.

THAT NIGHT over supper Lydia said, "Brother MacDowell is preaching tonight. It's Family Night." She saw that Haines's plate was nearly empty and automatically passed him the macaroni and cheese.

No one said anything.

Mary Ruth hated the way her mother said, "*Mac*Dowell," like a hick, an Okie with no schooling. She pushed the food around on her plate. The cat scratched at the back door and Mary Ruth went to let her in, then she sat back down, her ankles hooked around the chair legs.

"Cat's going to have kittens," Haines said.

"Yes, she is," Lydia answered. "In another week or so."

"Can't keep 'em all," Haines said.

Mary Ruth excused herself, cleared her plate and silverware from the table, and wandered into the living room. There was a picture of Jesus over the sofa and the eyes seemed to follow her around the room. She knew she would go to Family Night with her mother, but she wanted to let her worry about it.

She turned on the television to conceal the sounds she was making. She opened the wooden box and looked at the teeth. Her father had returned home two weeks ago, bringing with him the carved wooden box of human teeth, some brown with nicotine and worn, others small and perfect. There were two gold teeth, molars, glinting in the harsh light of the pole lamp beside the television. The inside of the box was lined with thin felt, the color of cheap lipstick, the kind her mother had worn before she became a Christian.

She had avoided Haines since he showed them the teeth. Avoiding him had been easy. She was at work all day. He stayed home all day, repairing locks, glazing windows – the house had been neglected in his absence – and making phone calls about work. He was retired from the army, but he was still a young man – thirty-eight – and wanted to work.

The war was on television. She was glad it was black and white and not color.

"Mary Ruth, I'll be ready to go in ten minutes," Lydia hollered from the kitchen.

Mary Ruth did not answer. She knew her mother still wondered if she would put up a fight. She went upstairs and changed into a skirt and blouse. She took down her braid and brushed her hair. She could just not answer and there would be no retaliation. Her father did the same thing to her mother. Half the time, conversations were begun and dropped by one person, for lack of answer. No one ever mentioned it.

Mary Ruth went downstairs and said, "I'm going outside to wait in the car."

Her father said, "I'll tell your mother. She's in the bathroom." He was watching the news, sitting in the rocker in his stocking feet, his blond hair in a fluffy fringe around his bald spot. He didn't look up.

VICTORY TEMPLE was across the river and east of town, a concrete block building always in some stage of construction. It was situated on a hill free of trees and studded with scab rock and rabbitbrush. The main room, the worship hall, was bathed in fluorescent lighting, lighting that left no softness, no ambiguity, no shadow but cleancut shadow. The ceiling made a curving arch, paneled in wainscotting. When she was younger, Mary Ruth had imagined it was the inside of Noah's ark, the belly of some salvation ship. She and Lydia scurried into a wooden pew halfway up the aisle.

The regular members of the church greeted one another with *Brother!* and *Sister!* Their hands lingered long in vigorous handshaking and the men thumped one another on the back. Many people carried Bibles, the men black ones, the women white. There were children, playing sly games when their parents' backs were turned, sticking out their tongues and pinching one another. Across the aisle and several rows ahead, Mary Ruth saw Franny squeezed between his sister Roseann and his mother, a chubby woman in a purple dress.

The service began with singing, the voices loud, accompanied by a woman playing the out-of-tune piano, a woman whose whole body entered into the act of making music, her shoulders rolling and dipping, her thighs bouncing on the piano stool. This was the part Mary Ruth liked best, singing the old songs, "What a Friend We Have in Jesus" and "This World Is Not My Home." Then one of the brothers, a man in a black suit, made a few announcements and asked for the offering. Wicker baskets were passed along the rows. Lydia laid a dollar bill in the basket, all the while keeping her eyes on the hymnal and singing, the knuckles of one hand white against the pew in front of her. During the offering, Brother McDowell sat a little to the side, up front, on a folding metal chair, scraping splinters from his thumb with a pocketknife.

Mary Ruth eased into a daydream of Franny's voice saying *sugar*. When she came away from the dream, Brother McDowell was preaching, speaking in a low voice, leaning on the podium, just like teachers in school. He might have been a teacher. He was good-looking, his brow clear and the hair at his temples graying in waves. He wore a suit of a material that looked dull in some lights and shiny with a slight turn of his shoulder, like the copper feathers on a pintail duck. He held a Bible in his hand and offered it to the crowd once in awhile, to make a point.

He was talking about living in the world and how hard it is to live in the world as a Christian. He was talking about indecency and Mary Ruth tugged at her short skirt. He specifically mentioned short skirts. He was talking about young people and freedom.

He pulled a clipping from his coat jacket pocket, and here, with a sense of the drama unfolding, Brother McDowell took the time to remove his coat jacket, slinging it over the folding chair. He gave the crowd a moment to stir and wonder. He came around in front of the podium, closer to them, and rolled up the sleeves of his white shirt.

Then he read the clipping to the crowd, a clipping about thirteen high school students in a neighboring town being arrested for skinny-dipping at the gravel pit. He read it with anguish, his voice growing louder and louder, blossoming into an embrace. His shirt was wet in half moons under the arms. His face was red, perspiring. He opened the Bible and read from it, a long passage, and when he finished, he said in a coaxing soft voice, "Come to Jesus. Rest in the arms of the Lord. Come right up here" – he spread his arms wide – "and He'll take care of you. Open your heart."

MARY RUTH started crying, not the kind of crying she could check, but tears she felt she'd saved for years. They flooded and rolled down her cheeks and she knew she had to go up front.

The pianist banged out "Washed in the Blood of the Lamb" and the congregation sang while Mary Ruth made her way, stumbling through the tears, to the front of the worship hall. A few others straggled up behind her. They knelt in a confused knot and Brother McDowell walked along, spreading his fingers on their scalps in a fervent touch.

"These people have come to the Lord. You can come, too. Open your heart to Jesus."

They sang "Amazing Grace" and Mary Ruth knew the service was over. Her mother came to her side and when she stood up her mother hugged her. Mary Ruth hated that hug more than anything. Her mother smelled like Lysol and the inside of closets in winter.

Afterwards, in her bed at home, she knew the feeling she had felt kneeling up front was the same one she expected to feel if Franny ever touched her. It was giving in, letting go. The preacher had said to her as she left the Victory Temple, "Jesus will walk with you."

It was Franny who walked with her, leaning protectively toward her, every day that first week of school. He would stand beside her locker and wait for her between classes. Sometimes the crowd in the hallway surged and pushed, throwing her and Franny close, close enough for kissing, but she always kept her arms curled around her books between them.

He asked her to go to the dance Friday night. She refused. Lydia would never let her go. Dancing was a sin. He asked her to go to the Victory Temple Sunday night and she accepted.

Lydia said all right, since it was church.

Sunday after supper he picked her up and drove to a dirt lane down the middle of a peach orchard. All the peach trees were growing in one direction, bound by the wind, despite the winter pruning. The wind off the river was stronger than all of them. The trees were black fingers in the blue night sky. There was a moon, slightly more than half full, like a tipped bowl. He didn't ask her if it was all right to drive there.

"I thought we were going to church," she said. Inside, she liked the feeling of being alone with him in the car, the radio playing, the upholstery cool against her arms.

"We'll get there," Franny said. "It's still forty-five minutes away."

He slid next to her, drawing her near. He was sucking on a mint she could smell. He had cut his neck shaving and the tiny flake of toilet paper he had placed over the cut was white bright in the dim car. She lay in his arms and let him hold her, the buttons on his shirt pressing into her cheek.

HAINES STARTED WORKING as the foreman of an apple orchard, four hundred acres of trees owned by a corporation in Yakima. He was seldom at home. Lydia went to the Victory Temple nearly every night. Sometimes Mary Ruth begged off, saying she had homework, and sometimes she went along and prayed and sang.

The nights she was left alone in the house were good. She began to keep a journal. She wrote down every exchange she had with her father.

> *He asked me how's school?*
> *I shrugged my shoulders.*
> *He came home drunk while she was at church.*
> *He said me and Lydia used to have fun.*
> *He asked me do you want to keep one of the new kittens?*
> *The gray one I said.*

While she wrote in the journal, sitting in the dining room near the gas heater, she listened to the FM station and smoked cigarettes.

One night, on the way to the Victory Temple, Lydia said, "Run in the store and get me a box of baking soda, Mary Ruth." She pulled over to the curb and dug in her purse for some change.

Mary Ruth ran inside, hair flying, and came to a dead standstill when she saw her father, his back to the door, his arm around Maggie, his meaty hand resting on her hip. Franny was there, shooting pool with a skinny boy in overalls. The woodstove gave off a powerful heat and the houseplants were like a jungle. There was a record playing, more static than music, an old Elvis Presley song. Franny sank the eight ball and crowed, his open mouth a circle of darkness. He moved swiftly to rack the balls again, saying without looking at her, "Hey, Mary Ruth. On your way to church?"

Her father turned, giving Maggie a quiet pat as he drew his arm away.

Mary Ruth could not look at him. "I'd like a box of soda, Maggie, please."

Maggie went behind the counter and took down the orange box and said, "Thirty-two cents." Her voice was soft as the light from the kerosene lantern hanging over the candy counter.

Mary Ruth skimmed across the floorboards toward the door. "I'll take you on again," she heard her father say.

That night she wrote in her journal: *His hand burns her. They have something.*

THE NEXT NIGHT she stayed home. She watched Lydia's taillights bounce down the driveway and down the lane until she turned onto the county road. She waited five minutes by the clock. Then she called Franny's house. She told his sister Roseann, who answered the phone, that she needed to ask him about a homework assignment. That was feeble, since they had no classes together, but maybe Roseann didn't know. She had been out of school for several years.

"Want to come over?" she said.

"What's up?" Franny said.

"Lydia's gone. I'm here alone."

"Sure," he whispered. "I'll be over."

They hung up and she took down the picture of Jesus and laid it face-down on the sofa. There was a clean rectangle of wall where the picture had been. She wrote in her journal: *He's coming over.* She wrote his name several times in a row. *Franny. Franny. Franny. Francis.*

It seemed his car crunched down the gravel driveway in a slow, cautious way. She watched through the crocheted curtains at the front window. He shut the car door, with only a quiet click of the lock, and walked to the house. She opened the door before he could knock.

"Come in," she said, giggling.

"You sure your ma's gone?" Franny said, looking around.

Mary Ruth danced around the room, feeling silly. "Sure, I'm sure," she said.

Franny sat down on the sofa, pushing the picture aside. "Look what I've got," he said, opening a plastic bag and offering it to her to sniff.

"What is it?"

"Dope, dummy."

He rolled a joint and they got stoned. Mary Ruth felt the music from the radio reaching into her ears. She sang along, forgetting she was at home, breaking rules. They ate a bag of gingersnaps.

SHE WENT to the bathroom and forgot to come back. After ten minutes, Franny knocked on the flimsy door, then entered the dark room, shadows from the light in the hallway cutting deep into the room. Mary Ruth stood in front of the mirror, the heels of her hands pressing on the rim of the basin. Franny walked behind her and crossed his arms in front of her, his hands resting, palms flat, on her stomach.

They stood like that for a few minutes. The new kittens meowed from a liquor box in the closet across the hallway. Franny unbuttoned her flannel shirt. Their eyes touched in the mirror. She began to shiver and buttoned her shirt, matter-of-factly.

"Did you see my father?" she said, leading him by the hand to the living room.

"He's at the store," Franny said, "telling war stories." They sat side-by-side on the sofa, kissing in their usual fashion, Franny chewing on her neck and earlobes, their tongues learning.

At nine o'clock Franny left. Mary Ruth went back to the mirror and turned on the bathroom light. Her cheeks were raw from whisker burn, her neck streaked with a long purplish bruise.

The next morning she smeared liquid make-up over the hickey. It was a bottle of make-up she had bought in sixth grade and never worn, a sticky liquid the color of twine. She put on a green turtleneck and a trench coat. The trench coat had a Coke stain on the sleeve and she wondered if Lydia would insist she wear something else. Haines's pickup swerved in the gravel; he was on his way to work.

"Mary Ruth?" Lydia's voice was high-pitched, almost a squeal from the kitchen.

Mary Ruth didn't answer. She looked out the window, chewing her thumbnail. It had rained during the night and the stone wall was slick. The pecan tree had lost its leaves in the wind. She was sick of hiding.

At last she went down to the kitchen. She hated its whiteness, its sterility. It reminded her of the dentist's office. There was an open green bottle on the back of the sink, its wick saturated with pine scent. She poured a cup of coffee from the percolator on the gas stove. She sat on a stool beside the window, pretending she was alone.

"Brother McDowell asked after you last night," Lydia said. She was unwrapping a package of frozen venison steaks.

"When I came home, the picture of Our Lord was on the sofa. Why is that?"

"I don't know," Mary Ruth said. She saw her reflection in the coffee pot on the stove. She pulled her turtleneck down an inch and tilted her head back, staring at the hickey.

Lydia turned from the sink. "Where did you get that?"

"What?"

"I know what you've been doing," Lydia said. Her voice was like a mallet in the room. Her face turned white, all the crow's feet and frown lines gray. She rushed at the girl, arms stiff, hands skeletal, and pinched her neck hard, screeching something unintelligible. She took Mary Ruth by the shoulder, bunching the trench coat around her face, and shook her until her head banged against the wall. Lydia was crying over and over, "What have you done to yourself? What have you done?"

Mary Ruth was limp and did not answer. She sat stock-still until Lydia slumped into a straightback chair next to the sink and laid her head down on the porcelain. Her hair was thinning on top and Mary Ruth could see her scalp at the part, pink as the inside of a rabbit's ear. Lydia took a flowered handkerchief from under her sweater sleeve and blew her nose and whimpered. Mary Ruth walked out.

She would never be like Lydia. She went down the hallway to the closet where the kittens lay curled with their mother. Their shiny eyes blinked when she opened the closet door and the light shone in the carton. The kittens meowed, a small noise, and wiggled closer to the mother cat.

Mary Ruth plucked the kittens from the mother cat's teats and put them one by one into a shoe box. They were awkward, bumping into one another and the sides of the card-board box. Their meowing grew more urgent. She carried them outside to the stone fence. It was a chilly autumn morning, with the smell of juniper smoke in the air. Some-one had raked the birch leaves into a wet, browning pile.

At the stone fence, she got rid of the kittens. She was very precise about it, using only enough force, a short controlled jerk of her wrist, to break the neck or back of each kitten against the stone fence. She killed them all, even the gray one.

Picking Time

REIN MEASURED sesame oil and vinegar into a pint canning jar, lifting the jar to the light to watch the oil separate from the red vinegar. Diane, his mother, made the salad, alternately tearing lettuce leaves and sipping mulled wine from a mug. Now and then she glanced at herself in the bamboo-framed mirror over the sink. The electric lights dimmed in collaboration with the wind.

"Your father wants it to be over," she said.

"So what else is new?"

"Rein," she scolded.

This kind of talk always depressed him, left him feeling disenfranchised. He regretted his smart-aleck tone, a remnant of his younger days. He was almost nineteen and learning to hold his tongue when necessary.

Diane let the cat outside. The weather stripping tacked to the bottom of the door scraped the linoleum and a small wind chilled the room. Rein shoved another quarter-log into the cookstove firebox.

"We're going to file for a legal separation," she said, matter-of-factly, and she faced him, arms folded, a lean woman in a caftan batiked with tiny blue threads of dye criss-crossing white hearts.

"I've heard that before," he said. He perched on the counter, wiping his glasses with a clean tea towel, his long, pale hair bound at the nape of his neck with a leather strip.

"This time we mean it," she said with a little laugh.

"I don't understand all this."

Diane lit the kerosene lamp on the warming oven, her back-up in case of power failure. "You can't call this a marriage," she said. "He's hardly ever here. He has a new life."

"I know. I know."

"Rein. Have you thought of what you might do?"

"Do?"

"I mean now that summer's over."

"You're talking goals, right?"

"You have Grandma's money. If you want to go to school."

"I don't know what I want to do."

"I feel like we made a mistake, bringing you here when you were so young."

"Mom, lay off the guilt. I might be just as confused if we'd stayed in California. I might be punked up on the street."

"I can see you in purple hair."

"What are you going to do? Stay here?"

"I like it here. If my work keeps selling, I'll be all right here."

There was a knock at the door and Diane threw up her arms in mock helplessness. As she was on her way to the door, Margo sashayed in, carrying a Coleman lantern.

"It's me," she said, slamming the door. "I'm leaving."

"You just got here," Diane said.

She was his mother's friend and Rein didn't know much about her, having relegated her to that nether-region of people who had close connections with Diane the nature of which he did not fully comprehend.

"I just decided to go apple-picking," Margo said, in a hoarse rush. "I know it's kind of late, late in the season, but I need the money and – " she paused and pushed her crinkly, wild hair away from her eyes, " – and I just want to get away. You know?"

She was the only woman Rein knew with a tattoo: a small blue cornflower next to the dimple on her shoulder. He'd seen it during the summer when she wore a ribbed white undershirt.

"When are you leaving?" he asked. Both women looked at him as though they had forgotten his presence.

"Tomorrow. I'm leaving tomorrow," Margo said. Her eyes were sooty-looking and she rolled her head around like a marionette.

"What can I do to help you on your way?" Diane asked, returning to the sink and the salad.

"Feed the chickens and hold my mail," Margo said, twisting a brown curl into a corkscrew with her forefinger as she talked.

"Sure thing. Is your pickup running okay?"

"Good enough," Margo said. "I still need two cords of wood."

"No rest for the wicked," Diane said.

"Goodnight, Diane," Rein said. He pulled on a stained down vest and headed for the door, his boots thumping on the floor.

"What about dinner?"

"It's okay. I need to think." He kissed her cheek and escaped the steamy kitchen.

The rickety porch creaked and the cat rubbed against his calf, arching her back, meowing. The night was clear and frosty, with stars pulsing in the sky. A half moon illuminated the footpath.

Rein followed the path down the slope to the creek, then crossed the sunken bridge and cut a diagonal through the alfalfa field. He liked to walk in the dark. At his house, a renovated woodshed, he stood on the porch for a few minutes and surveyed the sky and land, noting the dwellings across the canyon where lights flickered. He felt good, returning to the house he had made for himself, to his own private brand of domesticity.

Cold as a witch's tit. There hadn't been a fire since morning. He stumbled over something in the dark: hiking boots he had oiled earlier in the day. He lit a kerosene lamp and built a quick fire in the small airtight stove. His dry kindling started with a satisfying crackle. As the place warmed up, he stood at the window looking out and eating smoked fish and saltines and dried bing cherries. He considered going through his meager cache of skin magazines, but he'd been through them so many times, and they were only exciting the first time. He'd left his Ed Abbey book at Diane's and didn't want to go back for it.

He brushed his teeth on the front porch, spitting into the asparagus bed. Inside, he undressed and, in a whisper, cursed the oncoming winter. He gingerly crawled into the slick nylon sleeping bag, a bed which had been with him a long time and smelled of woodsmoke and insect repellent.

He lay in his bunk and his breath made quick pearls of warmth on the windowpane. The corn stalks were ragged, bleached in the moonlight. Feathery clouds drifted above the rimrock. The land, the light, the clouds seemed like a dream. He imagined he saw colors in the wind, and, almost imperceptibly, the golden autumn wind had changed to blue, the blue wind like a hungry coyote's cry, the blue wind glistening on snow. Who could he tell? Almost all of the people Rein knew had known him since he was ten years old. He was a kid to them. He never told them: *I built this house with my heart and hands, but now I have to leave it. I cannot sleep at night and lie awake waiting for something I cannot name.*

His parents were divorcing at last. He was the only remaining symbol of their twenty years together. His mother's wedding band, worn gold, was already lying at the bottom of a reed basket, along with her porcelain thimble and a few African trading beads. He didn't understand.

He felt adrift, without anchor. He'd finished his schooling by correspondence and that left him free, with a freedom that sometimes tasted like too much candy. He wanted to feel connected, to speak his truth to someone. He worked his way backward through a catalog of memories: summers when evenings stretched limitless before him, fishing at the lake, drinking home-brew with his neighbors, building campfires, sleeping late and washing in the creek in the mornings. He measured time by the summers, ripe and abundant. Ardent at last in the arms of sleep, he thought of going picking. There would be people there he knew, people his own age from other communities. He would hitch a ride with Margo.

"THAT EVERYTHING?" Margo asked, just before she slammed the tailgate.

"That's it," Rein said. "Sure this truck will make it, Margo?"

"Just get in," she said. "You have to get in the driver's side. The passenger door doesn't open."

Rein slid across the torn seat and Amber, Margo's two-year-old daughter, was jounced in next to him. She was a round, chubby girl in faded overalls and a blue sweatshirt, with a deep hood tied snugly around her face. In one hand she grasped a plastic bag of dried pears. Rein didn't speak to her; it didn't seem necessary.

"Okay," Margo shouted, "say your prayers to St. Christopher. We're on our way."

The truck was twenty years old and used a quart of oil every two hundred miles. The original paint was worn to a dull barn red, the roof interior stripped of much of its padding. The ride out of the canyon was shuddering and noisy, on gravel roads, but once on the pavement the truck settled into a rhythmic bounce. Amber offered him a dried pear and the sun was smoke-white in the sky. He began looking forward to the trip. They passed neat farmhouses and fields of barley stubble and Appaloosa horses.

"Want to smoke a joint?" Margo asked.

"After the crossroads," he said.

At the crossroads they stopped for gas at the U-Serve, U-Save. Margo pumped the gas. Rein checked the oil. Amber yelled, "I have to pee!" The woman in the motor home at the next gas pump – a woman with hair in tiny purple-white ringlets and pink cheeks in perfect clown circles – shot them a look of disgust, the lines above her upper lip deepening like scars.

On the road again, Margo slipped him a joint to light and pushed a cassette tape into the tape player. He didn't recognize the female vocalist competing with the truck's rattle. They shared the skinny joint as Amber watched them pass it back and forth across the cab.

When the tape ended they were passing through a flat town: two cafés, a dry goods store, a church and two taverns. Dust devils whirled among the sagebrush. Amber had fallen asleep, her head on Margo's thigh, her bare feet on Rein's. She made a connection between them. The miles rolled away and soon they were on the river highway, heading for the irrigated valley where orchards lay waiting, the dream site of fruit tramps tracking the mythical good picking.

"Why did you name her Amber?" he asked.

"My grandmother's name. I grew up with her," Margo said. "She was a tough old bird. With a heart of gold. A good woman."

He wondered at that expression, *a good woman*. What exactly did it mean? His father had said, when he left the canyon a year ago, *your mother is a good woman*. It had something to do with being virtuous, with not wanting to cause pain.

"Where was that? Where you grew up?" he asked.

"Miles City, Montana. Grandma owned a drinking establishment there."

"My grandma never touched a drop."

"Mine hardly ever did either. She sold it."

He shifted his weight and Amber stirred.

"Look at her toes," Margo said. "Like little sausages." She put on another tape: Pure Prairie League. "Tomorrow's my birthday," she went on. "I'll be twenty-seven."

"Happy birthday," Rein said.

"Wait until tomorrow," she chided. "I had a tarot reading done at the barter fair. Treated myself to it since my birthday was coming up. Did you see the man who was doing the readings?"

Rein shook his head.

"Strangest man. He had long fingernails and hair in a pigtail down his back. Charged me five dollars. We sat right in the dirt and he laid out a silk scarf for the cards. The scarf had a dragon on it."

"So what was his verdict?"

"He told me I needed to seek a balance in my life." She cocked an eye, gray as pepper, in his direction.

"Does that fit?"

"I told him my motto has always been *anything worth doing is worth doing in excess*."

Rein rolled down the window and breathed in the smell of sage. With one hand, Margo twirled her hair into corkscrews and drove on.

THEY FOUND WORK right away at Red Cheek Apple Orchard. There was a crooked row of plywood cabins, all occupied but one, and Margo and Amber moved in there. Rein erected a two-man tent on the hill above the cabins, a site sheltered on one side by aspen trees, with a view of the river and nearby town. They began picking apples at seven-thirty in the morning, had a half hour for lunch, and picked until five-thirty or six at night. Rein was averaging nine bins a day at six dollars a bin. The foreman, a thin man named Shuey with a gold front tooth, liked him and joked with him. The sun shone every day. As soon as he could he checked out the occupants of the other plywood cabins and was disappointed to find three families, another single man around thirty, and two weather-beaten fruit tramps in their fortieth season in the orchards. Old geezers, he called them privately. And then he spent several panic-stricken hours one night wondering if he would be an old geezer himself someday, with a hacking cough and shaking hands, the fingers cracked and swollen and split from some nutritional deficiency. The thought left him drowning in choices and he knew he was spending his last season picking. When he was younger, high school age, it had seemed okay, as though there was little else he could do for spending money. Now it hit him: he was here through choice or the inability to make a choice.

His days developed a pattern, familiar and comforting. Every morning he ate his buttered oatmeal standing beside a sage fire, elated by the rosy sunrise, the occasional wedge of geese in the sky. He wore wool gloves, a wool hat, and danced around the fire to stay warm. He pushed himself all day, piling up apples like money in the bank, beginning seedling dreams of what he might do after picking: hitch-hike to a warm sunny place in the southwest, or apply for a job in his favorite bookstore in Spokane, or visit his cousin Glynis in Seattle, a court stenographer who liked wild parties. Some days he was delirious with the idea that he could do anything, go anywhere, and this was a change from the sadness he'd felt at home, a feeling of homesickness before he'd even left.

His evenings were restless. He was hungry for something, for connection. He'd heard there was a large camp of young people called the Rainbow Family at the next orchard. Two nights in a row he walked the three-mile rutted lane, a tractor path, that would take him there most quickly. He hung around their campfires and watched the girls, all hippie girls, that's how he thought of them, in their heavy skirts and ribbed socks and bracelets made of leather and seeds. They had long hair and their breasts were loose beneath their sweaters. A few of the girls had babies and they nursed them openly. Rein watched, ravenous and a little ashamed, but not enough to stop watching. There was an easy kind of touching at this camp, hugs and swats and hand-holding. He wanted to be touched. But the circle did not open for him. He did not have the words to make it open. There was some trick to relating to people, some talisman he had not found, and he felt outside, invisible, and after the second night he did not return to their camp.

One night, by accident, he saw a girl bathing behind the cabins. He had looked out of his tent to check the progress of the full moon above the east horizon. She was standing in a zinc washtub, soaping all over, her short hair like a bud, the petals of a black flower curling on her scalp. Her body was slight but sturdy, and she soaped herself roughly. Her wet pubic hair looked silky in the moonlight.

He watched, entranced and hard, as the girl rapped on the back window of the cabin.

"Margo," she called urgently, "I'm ready."

Margo came around the corner of the cabin, dragging the garden hose provided by the owner for their bathing.

"Hurry. I'm freezing," the girl said.

"Here goes," Margo said, and she sprayed the girl all over with the cold water, rinsing her clean. A truck gunned by on the dirt road, headlights flashing, and Rein had the urge to protect the naked girl from the harsh light.

"I can see my breath," she said, huddling in a bulky robe and darting around the corner with Margo close behind. Her words came to him clear and true like bird sounds in the cold night.

He didn't sleep well after that, aching for the girl. The image of her bending over, soaping her thighs, stayed with him, returning over and over unbidden like a hologram in the moonlit tent.

"REIN? That you, boy?"

Rein looked down from the top step of his aluminum ladder, and through the leafy branches saw his father's face, brown as a walnut.

"How'd you know where to find me?"

"Margo wrote Diane."

Rein hung his canvas picking bag over a branch and climbed down the ladder. He and his father hugged one another, as they always had after long absences.

"How the hell are you?" his father said. And then, without

waiting for an answer, he held one arm toward a woman who had been standing around the other side of the tree. She came toward them.

"This is my new lady, Rein." His father took the woman's hand. "Jocelyn. We're on our way back to Mendocino."

"Hello, Rein," she said, and she was shy, holding his father's hand as though it would keep her from floating away.

"Hi," Rein said, hands in his jeans pockets. He wished he had seen them coming from a distance, to look them over, to prepare space for their existence in his mind. She was pretty, with straight blonde hair and green eyes, and young, maybe twenty-four. "Would you like some lemonade?"

"Sure," his father said, relieved, and they sank into the deep grasses and wild asparagus gone to seed in a smear of sunlight.

Rein poured lemonade into the thermos cap and offered it to Jocelyn. "Sorry I only have one cup."

"That's okay," she said, smiling. "We don't have anything contagious."

"How's the picking?" his father said.

"Not bad."

"Know what you're doing after?"

Rein shrugged. "Go back to the farm, I guess."

"We're building a restaurant," his father said.

"Natural foods," Jocelyn said. "You're welcome to come and work with us if you like."

They had talked it over.

"We'd like to have you," his father said.

Rein didn't say anything for a full minute. They each took a swig of lemonade. Finally he answered, "I might just do that." He knew he wouldn't. He didn't know exactly why, but he knew he wouldn't. "I'll think about it."

A tractor chugged down the row, noisy and smelly with exhaust fumes.

"I better get back to work," Rein said, standing.

His father stood up and gave Jocelyn his hand as she rose. She spanked her bottom with both hands, as though she'd gotten dirty.

"Come and see us, Rein," she said. "Anytime."

"Here's our address and phone number," his father said, handing him a green business card.

The tractor lumbered around them. His father shook his hand and said, "Take care. Keep in touch."

"You too," Rein said.

He watched them walk away, ducking branches as they went. His father had reverted to a former style, with neater clothes and shorter hair. *What goes around comes around,* Margo said. Now he understood the expression and he wondered if people aren't trapped forever in themselves, culturally stamped to be a certain way no matter how much they want to change. His father had been a fervent back-to-the-lander, in denim and manure-caked boots. The business card was the color of green apples. It read, *Bean Sprout Cafe and Pickin' Parlor. Eric and Jocelyn, Proprietors.*

"I THOUGHT I saw your dad's station wagon today," Margo said. She began talking even before she reached his camp. He was sitting outside against a rock, reading in the day's last light.

He placed a finger in the book to save his place. "You did. He was passing through."

"To where?" She sat down on a flat black stone and set a juice jar of tea between them.

"Mendocino." Rein drew a long swallow from the juice jar.

"Did he see Diane?"

"Margo, you already know the answers to these questions."

"I've got to get back to Amber. She's playing with the girl next door. Would you have dinner with us?"

"What're you having?" Rein said, grinning.

"Look. I'd like some company. There's this guy – Hemp. He's been after me sort of. If he comes around and you're there, he'll back off."

"Can I borrow your truck after?"

"Help me make the salad."

"Deal," he said, and he laughed and was surprised at the sound, he heard it so seldom these days.

After dinner Margo said, "I think I pulled a muscle today. Would you give it a rub?"

"Okay," Rein said. He piled the dirty dishes in the blue-enameled canner Margo used as a wash pan. Amber was asleep on an air mattress, snuggled in a sleeping bag printed with red and green cowboy scenes. It was windy and dark outside. From the next cabin they could hear the bluff and laughter of a card game. A television was on somewhere.

Margo sat in a faded canvas lawn chair, one hand on the muscle to the right of her blue tattoo. The yellow light of a sand candle wavered in the room. Rein used his thumbs as pressure points – a therapy his mother had taught him – and Margo squealed in pain.

"Too much?" he said.

"No, don't stop. If it hurts, it's good."

"Margo?"

"Yeah?"

"Who was that girl here the other night?"

"What girl?"

"The one who took the bath out back."

"Harder, Rein. She's from Appleland Orchard. Her name is Max."

He stopped working her muscle and pulled the light string. A glare flooded the room. "What kind of name is that for a girl?"

"Hey, I hate that light," Margo said.

He pulled the string again and the room was a cave of shadow. Margo stood up and did something she had never done before. She put her arms around his waist, slipped them surely around him and leaned toward him so that her crazy hair tickled his chin and cheek. She was short. He could distinctly feel one of her breasts against his ribcage.

"Margo, I have to go."

"If you gotta go, you gotta go," she said. She sat down in the lawn chair. "The keys are in the truck."

AT THE TAVERN he ordered a beer and no one asked for his identification. He sat at the bar and watched himself in the mirror and read the signs: *Sunday Masses, Immaculate Conception Chapel, 7:30 and 9 A.M.* and *All Deadly Weapons Forbidden.* The bartender kept an old potato chip can behind the bar and the men checked their knives as they came in. Long-hairs shot pool, while their women watched and gossiped and drank at the tiny formica tables lining the walls. There was a booth of Indians, seven crammed into the wooden seats that reminded Rein of church pews. The jukebox blared songs like "Ramblin' Man" and "Back on the Road Again."

Rein let the beer flow through him, ordered another quickly, and tried not to think about his father's hand on his new lady. It bothered him.

"Hey, Buddy, the next one's on me." It was an old fruit tramp who lived in one of the Red Cheek cabins. His face was misshapen and red, with rheumy blue eyes, a map of all the taverns he had rested in. He wore a shirt with pearl buttons and a string tie. His leathery neck was cross-hatched with deep lines, his hands knobby and scratched and nicotine-stained. When he talked his teeth protruded from his mouth, yellow as a horse's.

"Sure enough," Rein said.

The fruit tramp sat down on the next stool and raised his hand to the bartender. "You have a good day?" he said, his voice cracking like a trunk lid unopened for years.

"Nine bins," Rein said.

"I got ten." The old man cackled and the cackle turned into a ragged cough as he slapped his thigh. A cloud of dust erupted from his jeans. Then he hunched toward Rein in a confidential way. The can of snoose in his chest pocket bumped against the wooden bar. "I got ten bins and now I need to find myself a gal. To make my day complete. Know where a man can find a gal?"

"Sure don't," Rein said.

The bartender set two beers in front of them. While the old man was paying, Rein watched as Max swaggered in with another woman. They sat in the last empty booth, leaning across the table toward one another, lost in their conversation. Rein swung around on his stool, glass in hand, and pretended to watch the pool game.

"Had myself a woman once," the old man said. "We was married in Montana during cherries. Stayed together a long time. A long time." He took the snoose from his pocket, opened the can, and secreted a pinch inside his lower lip.

"What happened?" Rein said. Now Max was leaning on the jukebox, making selections, and tapping one foot in time to the music.

"What happened was this. She ran off with a foreman at a peach orchard down in California. Said she wanted to settle down and live out her days in sunshine. Left me a note."

Rein felt his bones softening and the rock and roll penetrating his brain like a drug. He bought a pack of cigarettes and lit one.

Max was greeting a lanky man, bear-hugging him. "Hemp," she said. "I haven't seen you in ages." They sat down together and Hemp put his felt cowboy hat with the curled brim on Max's head and teased her. Rein didn't want to watch, but he watched, drinking the beer the old man had bought him.

"That foreman had a Buick. Had a dent in the rear fender, but the push-button windows still worked," the old man said.

Max's woman friend joined a pudgy man in overalls at the pool table. Hemp's hand was on Max's hip. She kissed him on the cheek. A Mexican, his khakis torn at one knee, walked back to his booth from the jukebox, singing along with Linda Ronstadt.

"He had a trailer, too. A pink trailer with them Jap'nese maples in a row out front. A woman wants a house to call her own." The fruit tramp shook his head.

"See you around, old timer," Rein said. "Thanks for the beer." He pocketed the cigarettes, bought a quart of beer to go, buttoned up his wool plaid shirt, and left.

In the truck, he shivered and his hands shook as he started the engine. He had a little trouble getting the key in the ignition. The inside light didn't work and he fumbled with the headlight switch. His skin felt raw with cold and drunkenness.

He drove slowly and carefully out of town and down the river highway. He turned right at the Red Cheek sign and the truck fishtailed for a moment in the gravel.

He parked the truck, put the cold keys in his pocket, and stood outside for half a minute watching the stars roll in the sky. The cabins looked like dead jack-o'-lanterns in the night. The owner's house was a stone fortress farther up the road.

He knocked gently on Margo's door. In the blue moonlight, through the curtainless window, he could see her in her narrow bunk.

"Who's there?" she said, with a flicker of fright in her voice.

"It's me. Rein. Can I come in?"

He watched her get out of her sleeping bag and run her hands through her hair. She didn't have any clothes on. She opened the door and spied the quart of beer he carried.

"Brought me a peace offering, did you?" she said, ushering him in with a frantic wave.

When he stepped in his glasses fogged. She shut the door and slid the bolt lock over. He put one arm around her, pulling her near. She relaxed and pressed closer, kissing his chin.

"You smell like winter coming on," she said.

Friday Night at Silver Star

"I HAD my breasts enlarged last year," Elinor said, flipping down her rainbow tube top. Her hard, gleaming breasts popped out, like hood ornaments.

"They're nice," Jude said, politely.

Elinor sighed and flipped the tube top back up and huddled more snugly into her poncho. "They were good for a while. We had a lot of fun at first."

"Don't you now?" Jude said.

"Sometimes. I still like for Harvey to massage me with Abolene – that's the *preferred* lubricant of the cathouses in Nevada – did you know that?"

Jude shook her head.

"Harvey likes that. He talks to 'em, too." At this she grinned and her gold eye tooth gleamed in the moony darkness.

"That's kinda sweet."

"But it's like he's talking to *them*, not me," Elinor said. "He's talking to a couple of friggin' saline implants."

"How much did it cost?" Jude asked. She was finding herself more and more fascinated with how much things cost. Before she had any money, she couldn't have cared less.

"Twenty-five hundred. More or less." Elinor sighed again and took a short sip from the bottle of apricot brandy. "I'd of rather gone to Florida."

"Why Florida?"

"For the warm weather." She dragged out the word weather, exhaling, jutting her chin forward on the first syllable. "We could've laid on the white beaches at Port St. Joe and drank tequila sunrises. We could've visited my sister Pam in Little Rock on the way. Might have been just as much fun as new tits."

It was the first full moon in May and the cold light frosted the main lodge, the sheds, the gazebos housing the hot pools, the cars and trucks lining the muddy driveway. Jude could read some of the license plates – Foxy Lady, Warhead, Hyalite – from where she sat in the pickup, which was parked in its own personal ruts next to the sagging horse barn. She and Elinor had met a few hours ago, while poking through the potluck's remains, and now they were drinking apricot brandy, which was forbidden on Friday nights, and using up all Mason's gas keeping the heater running. On the tapedeck Bonnie Raitt was singing "Ain't Nobody Home." Up the road, in the crossroads town of Silver Star, there were no lights. There was something sneaky and adolescent and wonderful about sitting in the cab of the truck, drinking and talking in the middle of the night.

"This is your first time, isn't it?" Jude asked.

"Here," Elinor said. "It's our first time here. But we've been at it for a couple of years."

"How'd you get started?"

"We always did like to experiment. One thing led to another."

They sat in silence for a few minutes, and Jude wondered if she would plunge on ahead into talking or let it go. She felt like talking, like all the words, the disclosures, the secrets were waiting to spill over the dam of her inhibitions, her censor.

"How'd you get started?" Elinor said, just as the tape ended with a soft click.

The only sounds were the dry hum of the heater and the creek's metallic burbling just the other side of the horse barn. A man in running shorts came out the side door and took a leak right on Jude's daffodil bed. He pulled his elastic waistband down, just like a little boy, and whistled some school song Jude could hardly remember. "When Johnny Comes Marching Home Again" it was. It came to her just as the whistling stopped. He shook himself and went back inside, letting the screen door slam like a shot.

"Out of desperation," Jude finally said. "Mason bought this old hot-springs hotel thinking we could make a go of it. We're neither one of us business types, but we'd always had this dream about living in the country. Which is not all it's cracked up to be, by the way. This is a back road, case you hadn't noticed. There's hardly enough traffic to warrant plowing it in the winter, let alone support a business like ours. So Mason got the idea of having these Friday night potlucks. He calls it our low-overhead night. Our customers even supply the food." Jude laughed, shortly, abruptly. She drank from the fifth and felt the easy burn of the brandy going down.

"But how'd you get started participating?"

"It was a turn-on."

"Simple," Elinor said, giggling.

"A powerful turn-on."

"It's a good setting. The hot pools. The homey hospitality. Harvey and I have been to three other party places," Elinor said, authoritatively, "and none compared to this. It's worth the drive."

"You could write our advertising."

"Word of mouth, Honey. I'll advertise word of mouth."

"It was all those naked bodies did it for me," Jude said.

"I know," Elinor said. "Harvey and I used to be into skin flicks, but now, after the real thing, they bore me to death."

"So that's how we got started. That was ten weeks ago." Jude calculated: thirty couples a night times fifty dollars a couple times ten weeks. Fifteen thousand dollars. Not bad for an ex-horticulture student and a ski bum. She fantasized the hand-tooled maroon suede boots she was planning to buy on her next shopping spree.

"So why aren't you in there tonight?" Elinor ventured.

"I'm not sure," Jude said. "Maybe I just want to see if

Mason misses me. How about you?"

Elinor shrugged and lit a cigarette. "Harvey wanted me to get into a three-way with a woman I don't like."

"Which one?"

"The tiny blonde."

"Oh, her."

"You know the one I mean?"

"Julie. Of the Squeaky Cleans."

"That's the one."

"I don't like her, either."

"Why?"

"She's too cute."

"And stuck on herself."

"So you just said no?"

"I said, 'Knock yourself out, Sweetheart, but I'll take a raincheck.'"

"It doesn't bother you? To think of him – "

"Oh, yeah, sure, it bothers me. On some level. But not enough to stop him." She puffed two quick puffs on her cigarette. "When we first started we were into one-room encounters."

"Why'd you change?"

"It was too limiting."

"Mason used to say, 'It doesn't matter where you get your appetite, so long as you eat at home.' Looks like those days are gone."

"Harvey'll bring her home, too. Mentally. Miss Squeaky-Clean, I mean."

"That's one thing that bothers me," Jude said. "The rest of the week, it's like all these other people are in bed with us. Ghosts."

"Fantasies. That's what you're selling. Fantasies."

"So it's never just the two of us anymore."

"That's why we don't do parties very often."

"What's your zodiac sign, Elinor?"

"Scorpio. But I don't believe in it."

"Me neither, really."

From up in the foothills, a coyote yodeled. Jude handed Elinor the bottle and switched on the low-watt overhead light. She rummaged through the box of cassette tapes and selected one: *John Denver's Greatest Hits*. She slid the tape into the slot and it was in the middle of a song, "Take Me Home, Country Roads."

"How long have you and Harvey been together?" Jude asked, nudging off the light switch and settling herself again behind the steering wheel.

"Thirteen years," Elinor said, spunkily. "Harvey and I met in Las Vegas. He was a cab driver – that was before his brother offered him the partnership in the steel shelving business. I was a blackjack dealer. One night when I was on my break Harvey was there playing the slots and the money just came *pouring* out and Harvey started hollering *This thing's got the silver shits* and I got the giggles and laughed with him. We laughed until our sides ached. He was stoned on hash. And I thought he was the funniest guy. I took him home that very night and that was that. We got two beautiful girls. Sharleen and Dawn Beverly. Twelve and nine."

"When did you move to Missoula?"

"When Harvey went into business with his brother."

"You can't be a blackjack dealer in Missoula."

"I'm a part-time travel agent."

"You get to travel?"

"Mostly I work the office. But sometimes I get to go on fam trips."

"Fam?"

"Familiarization. So we can know where we're sending our clients."

"Where have you been?"

"Lake Tahoe. Hawaii. Once Harvey went with me on a ski trip to Sundance."

"How was it?"

"It snowed the whole dang time we were there. We sat in the lounge drinking rusty nails. Harvey tried to pick up this other couple, but it was no go."

"I met Mason at a ski lodge."

Jude helped herself to one of Elinor's cigarettes. They were the extra-long skinny kind. Elinor handed Jude the smoldering butt of hers to light up with.

"Finished?" Jude said.

"Ditch it," Elinor said.

Jude rolled down the window and flicked the red-tipped butt into the mud.

"Once I knew this guy named Skip," Jude said. "Dumb name, huh? Anyway, I knew him when I was just a kid. Nineteen. In college. He liked to go cross-country skiing. Once I went on an overnight trip with him. Into the mountains. The stars were so bright. We slept in a tent and had to melt snow for drinking water. We had to melt snow for drinking water," Jude repeated, amazed.

"Was he good? In bed, I mean."

"He was real nice. He played the harmonica." Jude hadn't

thought of Skip in years and she wondered where he was now. Was he still out in the pure mountains, naming the stars for some new lady?

"Sometimes I think I'd like to fall in love again," Elinor said.

"Yeah. I know."

Elinor leaned her head back against the seat and Jude said nothing more for a few minutes. She thought maybe Elinor was going to drift away – it was hard to tell in the semi-darkness. Someone turned off the front porch light and the kitchen light. The sky was paling just a bit and a few clouds streamed by over the mountains to the east. The wind must have been blowing hard up there. A snow plume rose and fell on the highest peak.

"Do you ever think of quitting?" Jude said.

"It'd be hard," Elinor said. "This is our lifestyle. I'd be afraid to quit."

"Afraid of what?"

"That it wouldn't be enough," Elinor said softly, her words as whispery as molted chicken feathers falling to the ground. "You know." She paused. "Just me and Harvey."

Jude had the impulse to reach out and hold Elinor's hand, but she couldn't quite bring herself to make the move. Somehow comfort was called for, but Jude felt inadequate to the moment. She thought Elinor might be insulted. So she handed her the bottle instead, saying, "Good to the last drop. Go ahead. It's yours."

Elinor tilted back her curly head and drank the last slug of brandy.

"What time is it, Jude?"

"Three-forty."

"Guess I better go check on Harvey. I need some sleep, too. Before the drive back."

"Will you come back?"

"More than likely." Elinor picked up her cigarettes and lighter, opened the door, slipped out and slammed it. "It's muddy out here," she said, but her words were muffled through the cab window and it seemed to Jude she was speaking from under water.

Elinor picked her way around the puddles toward the side door of the lodge. Jude switched on the dash lights and checked the gas. There was still a quarter of a tank. She crouched on the passenger side, pulled the back of the seat forward, and hid the empty brandy bottle behind there, with the oil rags and the tow rope. She decided to drive over to Three Forks to the all-night Grizzly Truck Stop on I-90. Her friend Lolly would be waiting tables the graveyard shift and she could have a slice of lemon meringue pie for breakfast and Lolly's fresh coffee. She and Lolly liked to throw the I-Ching when business was slow. Maybe later in the day Mason would take her into Butte to buy those boots. But she had to pass the time till then. The sky was a cottony gray now, but on the drive home from Three Forks the sun would warm things. The sun would wrap its sweet arms around everything. Maybe the trucker from Kansas City, Bobby Lee, would be at the Grizzly. Lolly had introduced them two Saturdays ago. Bobby Lee had called her Judith, *because it's so feminine*, he said.

Moving In

JOHN'S ROOM is across the hall from mine and he stops by late at night sometimes to see how I'm progressing. One stormy night I'm sitting in the dark watching the lightning in the eastern sky, and it's John at the door, bearing an eight-by-ten Maxfield Parrish print called "Ecstasy."

"My sister gave me this," he says, "but I think it suits you better."

I take the print and dart around the room, testing it against this wall, then that one, but in the dark I can't tell much. I don't want to turn on the light. "Thanks, John," I say, touched.

"I had it matted," he says, almost shyly, in his southern drawl. He pats the chest pocket of his white shirt and says, "Mind if I smoke, Laurel?"

"No, go ahead," I say, and I place the print, for safekeeping, on top of the wooden file cabinet. He's never stayed before. We sit in the dark, each of us in a rocker facing the windows, and John smokes and we still watch the lightning.

"Alexis came in tonight," he says. John waits tables at the Welcome Home Supper Club.

"How is she?" I say, light, lighter than a helium balloon, and I know I'm not fooling him.

"She looks ravishing, as usual," he says.

"What are you leaving out?" I say.

Pizza, John's calico cat, nudges open the door and comes picking her way around to us, first investigating a corner, then pawing the air near the telephone cord. She jumps on my lap and kneads my stomach.

"She was with a woman. Might have been her sister – they looked so much alike."

"Oh?" I am curious and ashamed of my curiosity.

"She said she wants to come and see your room. I told her how lovely it is."

"She knows where I live," I say.

Pizza stretches regally, bracing her front paws on the rocker arm and observing John. Then she springs toward his lap. That's where she really wants to be.

"Are you in love with her?" John says, stubbing out his cigarette in the ashtray.

"I don't know what that means," I say. I think he must be disappointed in my answer. The rockers creak against the wooden floor and we stop talking.

I am crazy about blue: cobalt, indigo, peacock, cadet. I paint the walls of my new room a color called Cove Blue. At night, in the dark, the room glows like a field of forget-me-nots in the high country. I plant phlox in a cedar tray on the mantle. John and I go to a country auction and I bid on an old blue-and-white quilt in a pinwheel pattern. One edge is singed – it has been rescued from a fire – but other than that, it's in good condition and makes me feel connected to a past I want to know. I want old things, quality things. So for two weeks, the room is my work. I move furniture, religiously go to garage sales, and throw out anything that doesn't belong in my new room: a starburst clock, earned with green stamps when I was twelve, a brown macramé wall hanging – dull as dirt – given me by Gregory, and a box of souvenirs from teaching, kids' drawings of me, valentines, a lopsided sand candle without a wick. The room becomes mine in a way no room has ever been. At every turn, I ask myself, what will make me feel good?

JOSEPHINE DRESSES in a ragtag assortment of clothing: flimsy rayons, bright flower prints, shirts with padded shoulders, mid-calf gabardine skirts that swirl around her chunky legs, hats with little veils from some 1930's detective film. While washing dishes together, I ask her what the style she dresses in is called. "Flashback," she replies, swiping a white plate with a dishtowel and clattering it into the cupboard.

"And the way Alexis dresses?" I ask.

"Minimal," Josephine says, laughing. "She's got the hips for nudity."

We first met, before the move, in the secluded backyard where Josephine lay spread-eagle on a Hudson's Bay blanket, wearing only sunglasses and multi-colored underpants printed with Minnie Mouse. She glistened with suntan oil.

"If you move in, this is one of the benefits. The privacy," she said. "I've always thought that brown fat is better than white fat. Like brown bread. Or brown rice."

Josephine is co-owner of a hole-in-the-wall bookstore, which profits well, or well enough. She furtively reads women's magazines, and knows the latest about the sun's effect on the skin and also that it is rumored an active sex life cures arthritis. She goes to A.A. meetings twice a week, matter-of-factly announcing, "I'm off to A.A. Catch you later." Josephine is obstinately cheerful, always on the go. We eat meals together sometimes, because our tastes in food are similar, running to spinach salads, falafel sandwiches, and only the occasional Oreo cookie binge.

"I have an idea for a business," she says one morning as we are unloading groceries and sorting them into cupboards. She has an idea for a business at least once a week.

"Tell me," I say, as I rearrange the vegetables in the crisper.

"A dating service," she says. "This town needs a dating service."

"For who?" I say. "University kids?"

"No, no. Not them," Josephine says, juggling three Granny Smith apples. Juggling is a skill she is perfecting, and she will juggle anything, anywhere, anytime. "For the newly divorced. Widows and widowers, maybe."

"Might work," I say, "but is it meaningful?"

"For Christ's sake, Laurel, who cares?" she says, stopping in mid-juggle, exasperated. One apple jolts to the floor, no doubt bruised, and rolls under the antique pie safe.

Her tone hurts my feelings. I close the fridge door and keep my back to her as I rummage further in the brown grocery sacks.

Josephine kneels down and retrieves the apple. I watch her from the corner of my eye and stifle the thought of kicking her big bottom. I hate myself for being so thin-skinned.

"Think about it," she says, leaving the kitchen. "We could be partners."

I MOVE IN during the sweet ease of summer. I am taking over the room of a woman named Alexis and our time in the house overlaps by seven days. I sleep in the solarium during that time, and no one seems to mind my being there—the solarium isn't used much, except, I discover later during my tenancy, for intervals of privacy: Josephine methodically laying out tarot cards for one of her friends, John and Piotr having one of their work-it-out talks. The solarium serves my needs, a square room with windows on three sides looking into the jungle of backyard. The floor tiles are chalky black ceramic and tomato plants in green plastic pots line one wall. The room is let go more than the rest of the house, with white wicker furniture coming unwoven at the corners and laces of cobwebs accumulating. I sleep on the floor on a Therma-rest foam pad, inside my new sleeping bag, which makes me feel like a silkworm or how I imagine a silkworm feels, producing all that lovely stuff.

I am moving in for a variety of reasons: for the company, to save money (I am between jobs and looking), and because I like the front door and covet it, want it for my very own, even if I am just a renter. The front door is walnut with a blue heron carved in relief.

I just moved out of a renovated school bus, parked on the hedged back lot of a friend's place, which I'd been sharing with Gregory, a computer science major, five years older than me and with a penchant for cocaine and magazines like *Hustler*. I'm a red wine drinker myself, which people like Gregory think is crude. If or when I look again, I want someone whose addictions I can share.

At any rate, Alexis feels the need to move out and I need a place, so it seems pre-ordained, part of the synchronitic domino effect of my life, that I will be welcomed into the house with the walnut heron on the door and three housemates who promise wit and a daily ration of hugs.

THE SECOND NIGHT we barbecue tandoori chicken on the back deck. John and Piotr, the couple of the house, orchestrate the dinner, John telling me when to turn the chicken as he plops mayonnaise into the potato salad, Piotr begging Josephine to change the music from Bette Midler to Bryan Adams, and all the while teasing one another, bumping bottoms with one another, mixing drinks. The kitchen smells like onions and John's little black cigarettes, which Piotr abhors. "Let me kiss your ashtray," he says, and then John offers his puckered lips in parody of some cartoon sweetheart. Piotr is brown and shirtless, in baggy gray slacks. He has a neat mustache, the whiskers several shades of gold and red. He teaches ærobics and I like the way he moves, like a dancer or a rock climber, with the grace that comes from using your body, all over, all the time. John is from North Carolina and speaks in a gentlemanly drawl, and his voice is soothing, a novelty, a comfort. He speaks often, more often than Piotr. He's short and compact in his white gym trunks and yellow T-shirt with *Rocky Mountain High* silk-screened on the front. He wears a silver ear cuff and his black hair is cropped very short, almost what we called a crew cut as children.

Josephine laughs with gusto at the two of them. "You guys are cute," she says, for no apparent reason other than her abiding affection for them, as she unstraps her black wedgies and tucks them out of the way into the kneehole of the kitchen desk.

I am feeling sort of at home, though I don't know any of them well. They don't ask me any questions about my past, preferring, I think, to plunge full-steam-ahead into the present. I have a mixed reaction: I'm relieved, since uncertainty plagues me, but I feel slightly left out, as though I want someone to ask just the pointed question, the momentous probe, which will reveal me to them. I want them to know me better than I know myself. I want them to be curious. I remind myself they're roommates, not therapists.

John, Piotr, and I sit down and unfold our paisley napkins. Josephine pours the wine with a flourish. The dinner – chicken, potato salad, sliced tomatoes, and corn bread – steams on the table. And then Alexis comes home.

"Drinking?" she says, from the doorway, and we all turn to her, surprised at the interruption of our party.

"Just pouring," Josephine says. "Being a good hostess."

And she sits down and forks tomato slices onto her plate.

"Join us?" Piotr says to Alexis, one arm raised, beckoning.

"I'd like that," Alexis says, her mood changing. At first she had slouched against the doorway, an outsider, her bright rose shawl artfully folded across one shoulder; now she seems almost childlike, eager to be invited, smiling as she ducks her head and looks at Piotr, her ally, sideways. I was always to be amazed at her mood changes, at her transitions from old, wise, worn to sweet, innocent, soft-spoken. I know nothing about Alexis when she enters the room. John has left her out of his thumbnail sketches of the house members. After all, she is leaving.

She throws her shawl on the sofa and scoots in between Josephine and John, patting their thighs as she settles in. John gets up and goes to the cupboard for another plate, into the drawer for silverware. I am introduced and she and I smile and nod to one another. We eat. We eat as though we haven't eaten all day, with relish, murmuring noises of appreciation with our mouths full, sighing and washing down corn bread with cabernet. But I am ill at ease since the arrival of Alexis. At first I think, I'm tired, I've had too much to drink, and then I realize I feel small, insignificant, with her there. Alexis is self-possessed, strong. She's tall and carries herself with a sureness, a lovingness. Yes, Alexis loves herself well, the sort of woman who touches herself often, running a finger along her jawline as she talks, massaging her own arms. Her shoulders are freckled. She wears loose cotton pants, the color of asters, and a white bandeau top. Her hair is long and black and crinkled, her eyes so dark it's difficult to tell the pupil from the iris. Her face is heart-shaped, with broad cheekbones and a tiny chin. These details do nothing to describe her. In spite of her good looks, her fire is what attracts and frightens me. She speaks as though all avenues are yet to be explored and celebrated, as though she can do anything and everything and survive.

I think she's overwhelming, peculiar. In high school, I might have described her as stuck on herself. The others treat her with a deference, a politeness they don't use with one another, as though she is some precious inheritance, a crystal wine glass that doesn't go with the other, cheaper, ones. Josephine notices when Alexis is eyeing the last bit of white meat on the chicken and says, "Go ahead, Alexis." And Piotr says, "I love you in summer clothes," completely out of context, since John has been discussing the relative merits of his grandmother's cooking and his mother's cooking and the recipes he has stolen from each. At Piotr's comment, Alexis squirms a bit, like a cat once petted who wants more. It is one of those small dinners where everyone must listen to everyone else.

LATER, when only a ragged carcass is left of the chicken, when John lights a cigarette and the stereo clicks off and the only sounds left are crickets, a circling sprinkler from next door, and a wind chime tinkling, Alexis says, "Well, Laurel, come up and I'll show you the secrets of your new room."

"What about cleaning up?" I say.

"Don't worry about it," Piotr says.

"The first meal's free, kid," John says, flicking ashes into his palm. "We'll get you hooked, then you wash dishes." He winks and I like the connection of that wink.

Alexis stands behind her chair, waiting for me.

"Sounds good," I say, accepting her invitation. Then I

stand there feeling awkward while she kisses John and Josephine both on their cheeks and then squeezes Piotr's hand across the table.

I follow her up the narrow carpeted stairway. Her room is in a turret on the second floor east corner. There are four windows that catch the morning sun, and Alexis takes full advantage of this with masses of houseplants, thriving on shelves in three tiers. One window has a deep window seat with soft cushions in jewel colors, emerald and ruby and azurite. There are books everywhere, and magazines, too, mostly literary journals I have seen but never read. I think: ivory tower. I wallow in martyr feelings. I'm good at this. I have been out there on the firing line, so to speak, working with children in braces and wheelchairs, and Alexis, in all her cool beauty, has been teaching part-time at the University. I question my choices for the zillionth time. She sashays around the room, lighting several candles, switching off the overhead light, turning on the music, plumping pillows, adjusting a windowshade, as I survey her room in silence.

"I just wanted some company," she says. "One to one." She pats the pillow across from her in the window seat and pours a tiny glass of some golden liqueur for each of us. From her tape deck, Alberta Hunter sings, "My man is such a handy man."

I accept the glass and the pillow, feeling shy, and scrunch my knees to my chest, blocking her. I feel taken over.

"So how do you like the house?" she says.

"I've admired the front door as long as I've lived in Bozeman," I say.

"It's a beauty, isn't it," she says. "Adar Tremaine lived here during the summers. She wrote some of her plays in this house." She sips from her glass and then returns it to the narrow ledge above the first windowpane beside us. The ledge is a sheet of agate suspended ingeniously with tiny-gauge chain.

"I haven't read her," I admit.

"I have two of her plays here if you want to," she says.

"I prefer novels. Big fat ones."

"Like those?" she says, pointing to a stack of paperbacks on the floor near a brown clay vase filled with straw flowers.

I nod.

"I devour those, too," Alexis says. "Especially when I want to get away."

"To get away from what?" I ask.

"From things I don't like at work. Or people. Or examining myself." She wears a silver bracelet, about one inch wide, engraved in some North Coast native design, and as she talks she slips the bracelet off and onto her slender wrist.

"Josephine tells me you've just quit your job," she says.

"That's right. I got so I hated to drag myself to work every morning."

"How long did you do it?"

"Four years. I'm thirty."

"We're all going through prolonged adolescence," she says, and she pours more of the lemony liqueur in my glass.

"How so?"

"Making decisions our parents made when they were twenty. You worked with kids?"

"Handicapped."

"And?" This is no casual questioning. She's waiting, facing me squarely, her legs crossed in a lotus position, leaning slightly toward me.

I tell her the whole story: the struggles with the teacher whose classroom I worked in, the way working with people who aren't whole depresses me, the way I berate myself for that depression, and, gradually, I warm to my own sad story and tell her about Gregory, the way I bounced back and forth all winter from the tunnel of school to the tunnel of the school bus, the kids with their unsolvable problems, Gregory in his California laid-back attitudes, which he wore like favorite clothing, never getting excited, never particularly happy or unhappy, lining up white threads of coke on a mirror as I stood at the postage-size stainless steel sink giving myself a spit bath, trying to wash away my discontent.

In the middle of my confessions, Alexis uncurls, stretches and stands up. I stop talking. "Don't lose where you are," she says. "I need to go to the bathroom."

While she's out of the room, I arrange the pillows on the floor and sink into them. It's dark outside. I have no idea of the time or how long I have been talking. Alexis returns and changes into a gauzy, rose-colored dress, and in a moment she is beside me on the floor, leaning back on her arms, palms flat. She's attentive again. I liked watching her change her clothes.

"You look lovely," I say, "and I feel like a grunt in these jeans and this T-shirt."

"Don't," she says. "That blue is a good color on you." And she lifts the hair from my forehead, stroking me. I feel like this is okay, but I wonder what might happen after this.

"What did you see in Gregory at first?" she asks.

"I think I liked his school bus more than him," I say, and at that Alexis laughs. "It seemed romantic, with its woodstove and the idea always there that we could run away, go traveling if we chose to. My life was so routine. I wanted the possibility of adventure."

"That's why I'm moving out of here," Alexis says.

"For the adventure?"

"Exactly. Here, I came to feel like the house, the people, satisfied me so much. I didn't seek out others. If I'm living alone, I'll have to reach out more."

"How long have you lived here?"

"Two years. I was here first, along with Piotr and John." Somewhere in the house a door slams. And then water is running.

"You and they were friends before?"

"John and I were lovers. Briefly." She rises and goes over to the tape player, and with one hand she presses the eject button, removes one tape, and replaces it with another, all the while running her other hand almost compulsively through her long hair, close to the scalp. More blues. She comes back to me and says, "I'd like to snuggle up to you." And she does just that, her back to me, her hair tickling my face.

"That was before John discovered Piotr. Or vice-versa. The three of us tried to be together for awhile, but it became obvious that they were the couple."

"How did that feel?" I say. I experiment with one hand on her bare shoulder. It's solid.

"Bad is bad," she says. "Then I just talked myself out of it."

I sit up and stretch, feeling stiff and cranky, wanting to go. Alexis rolls over, facing me, and makes low, growling noises in her throat. Her eyes are closed and with one hand she strokes my back.

"It's late," I say. "I'm going down to sleep."

She holds up her arms, her fingers wiggling, beckoning, as though for a hug. I'm standing beside her. "Good night, Alexis," I say.

Outside her door, which I shut much more loudly than I intend to, I feel sick. I sneak down the stairs for some reason. My face is hot and as I lie drifting in the moonlit solarium I keep seeing those arms, and I feel embarrassed, and I want to roll the scene back and play it over again. I want to hug her. I remember Gregory saying the only things you regret are the things you don't do. And I'm pissed off at her for her perfection, her dedication to style. I wish I had a cigarette, but I quit smoking five years ago.

I can't sleep. I get up and pad around the solarium for a few minutes, peering out the windows into the leafy darkness. I'm surrounded by cardboard boxes of my belongings, and they seem meager, like a refugee's lot. I go into the kitchen, thinking maybe John has left his cigarettes there. Piotr is there on the sofa, petting his gray cat, Silver Girl, as she lies perched on his thigh, claws retracted and purring. Her eyes look red in the lamplight.

"How's tricks?" Piotr says.

I say, "The inside of my head feels like a pinball machine."

Black Ice

THE FIRST NIGHT we met, Noah read my palm. We were drinking home-brew in his caretaker's cabin at Broken Heart Ranch. Dense snow fell outside and drifted in French curves against each single pane of the bay window. I'd been on my way to Jackson Hole, and the step-van had died just a mile inside the Park's boundaries. Noah had picked me up as I hitchhiked out of Gardiner, chilled in the early winter dusk, radiating my best non-verbal hitchhiking messages, smiles and thumb held high, just playacting, because I was plenty pissed about the step-van. It was parked in the gas station across from the fly-fishing shop, void of life as a block of ice. Noah eased my silver rings from my fingers and lined them in a row on his pine table. He held my hand just inside the circle of light cast by the Aladdin lamp.

"You don't have much to worry about," he said, "except what's in your mind." He kneaded the heel of my weather-rough hand with his thumb. "Your love line's broken several times. You'll eventually be successful in work. There's a major fork in your life in your fifties. Wonder what that can be?"

"Can't you tell?" I said, more harshly than I'd intended, pulling away.

"That's not the way of palmistry," Noah said, leaning back into the flexible weave of his willow brush chair, one hand tucked under his armpit, the other stroking his spirally black beard.

I played with my rings – a thick plain band, a pinkie ring of thin silver wire, an agate, and an elk's tooth on a crusty abstract setting – nudging them around the tabletop like game-pieces. Four rings, each with its own story. The silence in the cabin was the sort that works just fine. People in cabins out where the coyotes howl, under mountain shadow, away from town lights, know certain silences are inevitable and that there's no filling them. Quiet times are not like empty beer pitchers.

"What'll you do about your vehicle?" Noah said, getting up to slide another log in the stove.

"Have it checked out by the mechanic at the gas station. If he can't fix it – and that's likely – I'll have to tow it back to Bozeman."

He opened and poured another quart of home-brew, handling the brown labelless bottle like a sleeping baby, to keep the dregs settled on the bottom.

"Good beer," I said, wiggling on my rings.

"Arlene and I made this last spring." Arlene was the sole proprietor of Broken Heart Ranch and the Broken Heart Antique Shop, and Noah's boss.

"What's she like?"

"Arlene? Her claim to fame's winning a wet T-shirt contest at the Sundance ten years ago. That, and saving the ranch from subdivision."

"Is she around?"

"Never in the winter," he said. "Her sister has a condo in Pensacola."

"She trusts you."

"I'm trustworthy," he said, smiling.

And so he seemed. We weren't true strangers. I'd seen him in the K-Bar last summer, making eyes at the bartender, a woman named Nancy, who drove bus for a rafting outfit during the day. He'd had a good tan then, brown as seven-grain bread. I remember I noticed his forearms and his grace, a certainty in his walk, an animal spring when he prowled around the pool table.

"You lived in Bozeman long?" he said.

"Off and on for a long time."

"By yourself?"

"Rarely."

"I'll come right out with it," he said, smiling again. "You

have a partner?"

I nodded. I didn't say her name. Montanans are slow to come to bisexuality, right behind Idaho and Utah. He didn't need to know about Ramona just yet, especially since I was so unsure about Ramona. We'd lived together for three years, over the Leaf and Bean Coffee Bar on Main Street. For the last six months, we'd gone from bad to worse. No love-making. Ramona losing weight like a hand-me-down she wanted to discard. Her hips gouging me when I tried to hug her. I'd met her at the Filling Station one afternoon when I was waitressing and she was setting up amplifiers for a band called Final Exam. We clicked. What can I say? It lasted. One conversation led to another, and before long we were stir-frying vegetables on the gas stove in the step-van, by the smelly light of a kerosene lamp. She had a good mind, a most endearing laugh, and her voice was smooth as cheese-cake, sweet and proper. Her breasts were beautiful. And also her cheekbones. In the three years we'd lived together, her blonde hair had gone through several metamorphoses: long and ragged when we met, then cut to within an inch of her scalp all over, and now a little longer, with a flamboyant forelock over her eyes she could take refuge behind. She was twenty-four then. Born in Townsend, Catholic, sixth in a family of nine, and with a yellow sign in the front yard on Highway 12 which read *Stop government waste...pay taxes on election day*. She'd never gone to bed with a woman before.

"Where were you headed?" Noah said.

"Jackson Hole. Some friends are setting up a yurt system for skiers. They asked me to help."

"Looks like they'll close the road early."

He went to the cupboards and arranged a plate of food,

sliced pears, Boursin cheese, and Triscuits. We ate with relish.

"But things're not right with me and my partner," I volunteered.

"That's too bad." He pressed his index finger into the wheat shreds left on the plate and then licked his finger.

"It sure is."

That seemed to be all he had to say on the topic, and certainly all I had to say. I wanted to kick myself. I couldn't tell what he was thinking and I wasn't sure what I was thinking. I hadn't been alone with a man in a long time.

"Listen, Roxie. We could bring your van back here tomorrow. I could take a look at it."

"You're a mechanic?"

"I do a little of everything."

"I don't want to take up your time."

"I'd like to help you out."

"Let's see in the morning," I said. "Maybe it's something minor. Maybe it's healed itself overnight."

He laughed. "Could be," he said, standing and stretching, his muscles rounded and substantial beneath his navy turtleneck. "I'm going to sleep now. The sofa there's soft and wide."

"I have my sleeping bag," I said, stooping and clutching it to my chest like a worn teddy bear.

"That pillow – the flowered one – " he pointed to the end of the sofa – "has a dream cushion inside. Filled with mugwort."

"What's that?"

"An herb. Sleeping next to it will intensify your dreams."

"Oh yeah?" I said, still clutching the sleeping bag.

"Works for me," he said, setting the empty plate in the sink. He walked to the loft ladder and started up, but stopped on the second rung. "Will you blow out the lamp?"

I sat on the sofa, nodding and skinning down my knee-high, powder-blue knicker socks. "I have this uncanny ability to know – right away – when a person I meet is going to be significant to me," I said. "The curse of synchronicity."

"You met your match, kiddo. I'm psychic down to my toe jam."

He went on up. I blew out the lamp, stripped down, and crawled inside my sleeping bag. There was clean laundry, pungent with detergent, in comforting, clumsy stacks on the back of the sofa. I smiled to myself in the dark, maybe for the first time in months. My last thought was my mother's voice saying *never take rides from strangers.* I sank into the featherbed of sleep, the silence of the cabin a mix of wind and sparks and creaking walls.

OCTOBER had not been a good month. Barrel-fisted and a little drunk on river wind, the Montana winter bickered with autumn and autumn let go, backing out the door with no gumption. The cross-country skiers rolled up and down the cold twilight streets on their ski-skates. I didn't need the reminder of the season. The people who believe in snow's magical properties pointed to the Bridgers and Spanish Peaks, collecting rumors about winter. Snow took the high country in bondage, flushing elk down to forage in the valleys and face the hunters. I was still unemployed.

A week before the Jackson Hole trip took hold of me, my younger sister, Jan Mary, had called at midnight Montana time to say our brother Christopher was in the psychiatric ward at Emmanuel Hospital. I shivered at the kitchen table. On the second floor of the building across the street, the blue neon dentist's sign flashed the word *smile*.

"Let me get a blanket before you tell me about it," I said. I hurried into the bedroom and snatched a quilt from the bed.

She said, "He's been having these paranoid delusions for awhile. Nobody took them seriously."

I said, "There's a history of ignoring these things in our family."

"He quit his job," she said, "and moved to Ashland with another woman."

I'd been drinking red wine and my skin had that raw feeling, like the first layer's been peeled away. Ramona wasn't in yet. I shivered the whole time we talked.

His hospitalization left me walking around in my vulnerable shoes. I always expect the worst in any situation, one of my mother's lessons. If I swallow a vitamin when I'm alone, I'll choke. If I'm driving in winter, I'll hit black ice.

THE NEXT MORNING Noah made pecan pancakes for breakfast while I stayed snug inside my sleeping bag and watched. The sun was shining. Chickadees taxied around the feeder on the back porch. Noah whistled some Lightning Hopkins song as he hustled around the kitchen, full of energy, almost childlike. I wasn't used to it. Ramona had been taking two hours to rouse herself out of bed in the mornings, first smoking a few cigarettes, reading awhile, then testing the day by raising the blue paper shade just enough to check out the weather.

At breakfast we talked. He poured mugs of Mexican Pluma

coffee and we talked about substance abuse versus judicious use: caffeine, nicotine, alcohol, grass, toot, speed, acid, mushrooms. He said he had some mushrooms.

I said, "Remember black flats?"

He said, "Remember black beauties?"

We laughed and agreed those were crazy times.

"I could go for more crazy times," he said. "Some winter nights, at any rate."

"How old are you?" I said.

"Thirty-nine. And you?"

"Thirty-five."

WE DROVE up to Gardiner in his well-preserved '65 Dodge pickup. Traveling south through the valley, he pointed to the avalanche-marked mountains and named them. The sun glare was intense, the snow glistening. He was all weather and animals and geology as we drove, and I thought how different men are. They are such surface swimmers, strong and knowledgeable about the outer world, and once in awhile they dive deep into the unknown sea of feelings. It's like they can't stay down there too long. I didn't know if I could either. The night-long, sad talks I'd had lately with Ramona were wearing me out. I'd drag myself through the next day like a dead woman.

Noah took ten minutes to determine that there was something wrong with the fuel pump in the step-van, that he had the parts in his private junk yard back at the ranch, that he would tow me there. I allowed him to make these decisions. He asked me to go to the grocery and buy sour cream and an avocado. I ran this errand while he prepared the van for towing.

Alone in the step-van, on the way back to Broken Heart, I had too much time to think. I thought about Christopher in the hospital in Portland. A stupid phrase – *they're dropping like flies all around us* – kept running rat-like in my brain. I actually saw the words, like the credits of an animated cartoon.

The night Jan Mary had called, Ramona never came home. I didn't sleep well and finally dragged myself out of bed at seven the next morning while the AT&T rates were still low. I phoned Christopher at Emmanuel Hospital, getting cut off repeatedly because their switchboard was on the blink. I persisted until we had a good connection.

He said, "I can't read. Can't do anything in this place. I have two books. One on family politics. And one on love."

I said, "Has the doctor given you a chance to talk about what's bothering you?"

"Not really," he said.

We talked about what went wrong with our romances, our relationships. This could have taken hours, but over the years we'd each created a concentrate of what went wrong, distilled into a few sentences, some silence. Had we not been talking long distance, we might have reconstituted what went wrong and talked all day, breaking only to go out for a bottle of gin when it was respectable drinking time. I might have given him my most recent installment of life with Ramona. As it was, we hung up when my bran muffins came out of the oven.

BACK AT BROKEN HEART, Noah said, "How about making some guacamole and chapatis while I work on the fuel pump?"

I agreed and he went whistling to his tool shed. It was like playing house. And not unpleasant. I pretended he was my sweetheart for a few minutes. I started a fire in the wood cookstove and when it got going, I made some hot sauce from a pint of his canned tomatoes. He came back in, his hands streaked with something gray. He washed them at the sink, then heated some leftover chili. We baked the chapatis directly on the black stovetop, and filled them with the chili, sour cream, and guacamole.

I liked looking at him, I decided, as we sat eating at the sunny pine table. There was a peace about his eyes, like he'd settled up with himself, a long time ago, and was content. His hair was glossy and dark. When I thought he wasn't looking, when he got up to get something from the cupboard, I drank in the way his faded jeans fit him, loosely, but so his leanness was evident. We focused on the food and it was difficult to make eye contact. Some questions had begun to form there.

"Want to eat those 'shrooms after I finish the fuel pump?" he said. He was friendly, generous. No pressure.

My heart leaped around like a deer on opening day of hunting season.

"Sure," I said, before I could stop myself.

"I know where there's a hot pot. Two miles up the gulch. We could walk up there and soak."

"Sounds good," I said. I knew I was being incongruent. This was a word Ramona had often used to describe me, a word she learned in her sexuality support group. A fancy way of saying I think one thing and say another. But the hot pot did sound good. The part I left out was my fear. Incongruency by omission.

He finished the fuel pump. I straightened the inside of the

cabin, since order makes me feel better when I'm coming down.

He kept the mushrooms in the freezer of his propane fridge, in a lumpfish caviar jar from Teaneck, New Jersey. They looked like tiny pieces of twisted driftwood. He divided them between us, *one for you, one for me*, until we each had a small pile, and when I began chewing them, I immediately felt a portentous shiver from the back of my throat down my spine. We organized our rucksacks for the walk: two apples each, a bag of gorp, pocketknives, matches, bath-towels.

He knew the way. We wound around the south side of Dexter Point, on a sheep trail, and the hoof prints in the snow were like crystal prisms. His Vibram soles made waffles and I followed, gradually feeling the 'shrooms take hold. We entered the dark gulch and followed the stream, which was sharp with ice. Yellow cottonwood leaves littered the new snow patches. I felt a scary surge of energy, like the laceration of a caul, an opaque membrane, over my mind and senses. No defenses. I was afraid I would think too much about Ramona and her new lover, about Christopher not being able to read his new book on family politics, about the way he might lie there in the hospital dark, feeling the sorrow of being alive.

"Noah?" I called softly, stopping on the path.

He turned around in slow motion, his teal blue sweater filling up my eyes. "What is it, Roxie?"

"I've only done this with friends before." The sound of the creek's burble was large in my ears, as though I might be going underwater.

He walked over to me and put his arm around my shoulders. "Let's be friends, then," he said.

I smelled him for the first time, and he smelled of woodsmoke and Dr. Bronner's almond soap. His kindness made me cry. I felt layers and layers of emotions: stupidity, embarrassment, gratitude, regret. I was like a mad woman set loose in the elevator of a horror-house of emotions, not sure which floor I'd end up on. I finally settled for regret. I thought I'd made a mistake, eating the 'shrooms. That's the worst thing you can think once you've ingested them. It's one of those no-turning-back situations. You have to make the best of it.

"Look," he said from behind me, one arm over my shoulder, "there's one of my favorite trees." He was quiet-spoken, as though the trees might bolt and run. His favorite was an ancient, twisted juniper, the branches tangled to the ground, making shelter.

I stopped crying. Tears on my face were icicle stripes.

"It's beautiful," I said. "I had one like it as a child. I read under there to escape the heat of summer."

Noah turned me around and gripped both my upper arms through the bulk of my green down parka. His face was mobile and gentle, and I thought I saw the face of a teacher I'd once loved, and an older cousin, who'd been a man when I was a girl, and who once shared his art materials with me.

"Are you okay?" he said.

I was tongue-tied – how could I tell what golden light, what disgust was set loose with all my memories? I nodded and we walked.

"We're still on Arlene's land," he said. "That lady has *mucho* bucks."

"I called Ramona a slut," I said. It just popped out. Oh shit, I thought, now I'm about to spill my guts.

"Who's Ramona?"

"My lover. Ex. As in exit."

He just kept walking, his size-twelve boots crunching in the snow. "Want to tell me more?"

I told him about the good times, the wanton times. The way we used to drink café mochas in bed on Sunday mornings, reading aloud the record reviews and funnies. About our trip to San Francisco, where we could freely walk down the street, our arms around one another.

We were breathing hard from the uphill climb as we reached the hot pot, a sidestream dammed with stones and railroad ties. A rusty iron pipe, embedded between two ties, kept the flow clear and clean.

Noah laid down his rucksack, sat on a flat stone, and began untying his boot laces. "That's the saddest thing," he said. "When love reaches that point."

"What point?"

"Where you're calling one another names."

I undressed. I wasn't shy of him – since we'd talked. The snow was rough beneath my bare feet, and I quickly moved to the cushy moss surrounding the hot pot, the area so near the heat that snow never lasted there. We slipped into the steaming water, which was slick, as though it had a high mineral content. I sat down, leaning back on my elbows, and was in up to my neck. It was a two-person pot, about three times the size of a bathtub.

"Earth to Roxie. Earth to Roxie," Noah said.

"I'm here," I said.

"Where'd you go?"

"My brother was just released from a psych ward," I said. "I think about him."

"You've had it tough, lady."

"Jackson Hole was looking good – just to get away."

"I've tried that tack. Distance yourself geographically. Works for awhile."

"But not for long?"

"What do you think? This isn't your first time."

"I'm tired."

"Tell me about your brother."

"It's a chemical imbalance."

Noah ducked his head underwater for a moment, then relaxed, stretched out, his penis, knees, and the slight round of his stomach out of the water, his hands sculling. He waited for me to go on.

I told him the story. How the week Christopher was in the hospital, I was on the phone long-distance every day. The bill hadn't come in yet. I talked with everyone in my family. We'd all taken his hospitalization as a blow. There were so many things we wanted to forget. Jan Mary and I said, *it could happen to him, it could happen to me,* and we laughed when we said it, sick at heart.

"How old is he?" Noah said.

"Thirty-four," I said. "It's taken mother's chickens twenty years to come home to roost with him."

BACK AT THE CABIN, we were still high. The interior swirled and pulsed like a Van Gogh print. Before we made love, I told Noah how every evening when Christopher and I were in high school, when we lived in the Washington countryside, on the edge of an apple orchard, we'd walk to the store down the road to buy a city newspaper. We were political in those days, when there was still time to make change. Sometimes we spoke only Spanish during those walks. We shared a fantasy about moving to Central America when we graduated. He was sweet on a girl named Serena Davis, and he gave her a dozen red roses when she starred in the school's production of *Oklahoma*.

"How is he now?" Noah said, tucking my hair behind my ear.

"The day he was released, I called him again. He sounded subdued from the medication. He said, 'I'd sure like to have a visit with you. I'd cry for the first half-hour, but then it'd be good.'"

Noah said, "Don't cry. You're pretty."

In the moon-soaked dusk, his eyes were closed and I hoped he'd keep them closed. Too late, I realized there was no cure for what ailed me outside myself.

Incongruent to the end, I teased, "I bet you say that to all the girls."

As Luck Would Have It

SUNBOW NEVER KNEW what hit her. Kelsey rode over from the cattle ranch bordering our land, rode over on a white horse named Shasta, and Sunbow was in love. We laughed about that later – a regular knight on a white horse, Kelsey.

His full name was Obadiah T Kelsey. There was no period after the T because it didn't stand for anything. It was just an initial he had given himself when he was partners with a hunting guide near Woodpecker. He let it be known he was just biding his hard times until he could return to the good life farther up north. Cattle ranching was too civilized and settled for him. Kelsey was six-foot-four, a strapping man, with a face as eroded as the draws during spring flood. His hair was white and thick, his eyes blue as glacial ice.

I was there, in the garden, when Kelsey rode over on a sunny day toward the first of June. Sunbow, Little Egypt, and I were planting corn in long crooked rows near the road. We were barefooted and bare-breasted.

"Scuse me, ladies," Kelsey said, touching his stained felt hat in an abbreviated gentlemanly gesture, "where can I find Virginia?"

"I'm Virginia," I said, wiping my hand on my skirt and reaching to shake his hand.

"My name's Kelsey," he said. His voice was sure and slow, a baritone, and made me think of malt syrup pouring into a batch of beer. "I'm working for Mr. Giles. He asked me to tell you we'll be runnin' cattle through here tomorrow." He did his best to keep his eyes riveted to our faces. His horse was a sleepy, placid fellow, his forelegs muddy. Shasta had been the hired man's horse as long as I could remember, fourteen years or so.

Little Egypt turned her back, picked up a rusty rake, and moved to another section of the garden. I threw on a chambray shirt.

"Tell Mr. Giles I said thank you for warning us," I said.

Without another word, Kelsey reined his horse around and rode away down the gravel road. Sunbow stood there, watching him until he was a white blur against the mud and pine trees. I could see the winter alone had been hard on her. She had a hungry look in her eyes.

The sun came out again. I planted half a row of corn and covered it before Sunbow returned to work. She bent over the row next to me, her braids and breasts swaying, and nudged the seed corn into the damp earth, following the shallow trough Little Egypt had made with the handle of the rake.

"Who was he?" she said.

"I'm heading home," Little Egypt hollered. Her baby, Jade, was due to wake up from her nap. She waved from the old squash bed. We waved back. Little Egypt was young, only twenty-seven, and suspicious of men. She was beautiful was why, with skin brown as bracken fern in autumn and eyes the color of early peas.

"New hired man, looks like," I said.

"I liked him," Sunbow said. She patted dirt over the row.

"I could tell," I said.

"What do you think he was thinking?"

"I think he thought he was in hog-heaven."

SUNBOW WAS over Roger. He left for good summer before last. Out here, most folks find a mate for the winter, someone to share the chores, the wood chopping and water hauling, someone to warm the bed during the long nights. After Roger left Sunbow was too crushed to make the effort. She spent the winter alone in her A-frame, sleeping by the fire and waking during the night to write down her dreams in a leather notebook. She grieved and her hair grew a little gray and she went to town only once to buy supplies for her jewelry-making.

And then, Kelsey and Sunbow began to keep company, two independent spirits sparking like matches on rock in the magic of the weather, the lengthening daylight. It wasn't long before Kelsey was spending the night. If Gabe Giles minded his hired man staying the night at our place, he kept it to himself. He knows good help in these distant parts is hard to come by and harder to keep.

Sunbow began the habit of rising with him and cooking his breakfast over a firepit near her front porch. She didn't want to heat the house with the cookstove. I would see her, on my way to the cow barn, squatting in the yard dirt, her hair disheveled and eyes puffy with sleep, in a washed-out nightgown of an exotic Indian print, long worn thin enough to read a newspaper through, and she was lovely, feeding small strips of kindling to the fire. After she got it going a little, she walked around the yard, grasping her gown in one hand to form a bowl, and gathered pine cones and chips of wood and dry grasses, like some peasant woman. Sometimes if Kelsey was still in the house I stopped and talked with Sunbow while she made the coffee. Her pot was ash-black and she made the coffee strong. The light in her eyes was new and not new. I'd seen her fall in love before.

On my way home from milking I gave them a quart of milk. Kelsey loved the cream. They had an old overstuffed chair in the yard, a chair that looked as though it had sprouted there like a mushroom. Kelsey sat there eating while Sunbow perched on the arm of the chair. When he'd finished his eggs and hash browns and a second cup of coffee, then Kelsey braided Sunbow's hair. I saw all this from my kitchen window.

She sat between his knees like a child. He brushed her long black hair with a boar bristle brush he had given her. His hands were large and hammy against her scalp, but Kelsey braided hair as though he had done it all his life, gently and evenly. They made quite a picture, two lovers in the pearly curve of early sunlight, the fire smoking beside them.

SUMMER WENT ON like this, days and days of the purest sunshine and cloudless skies. We harvested the early peas and rhubarb.

"I want to go on a fast," Sunbow told me. We were sitting on her porch, in the shade, cutting stalks of rhubarb into chunks for wine. My bare legs hung over the edge of the porch and a dampness from the crawl space under the house cooled me. Sunbow wore a ragged straw hat with a cheesecloth veil to keep the flies and mosquitoes away.

"When's this take place?" I said.

"I'd like to go into the woods tomorrow. Would you take me?"

Now it is Sunbow's ritual to have a friend take her to the woods once in the summer, confiscate her shoes, and leave her there to fast and weep and sit by the fire. For three days and nights.

"Why not let Kelsey ride you up there on Shasta?" I said.

"Kelsey won't do it," she said. "He thinks I'm crazy."

"Oh?"

"He's just never heard of such a thing," she said. Then she put down her paring knife and with both hands curled back the cheesecloth veil. "We're starting to spar," she said.

I jumped down from the porch and hoisted up another wicker basket of rhubarb. "That's inevitable," I said. "The fall from grace."

The next morning, early in the clinging fog, we trudged the dusty trail that switchbacked up the canyon wall and into a small wood of birch and larch and aspen. A flicker of a stream ran through there, but the water was not good, contaminated by cattle farther up. Sunbow had brought only two quarts of water to last the three days. I left her in a grassy clearing dimpled with the beds of deer. She was moving stones to build a fire ring, singing some chant as she worked, her voice low and clear.

Much to my surprise, Kelsey came to see me that evening. He looked a little down in the mouth and twisted the brim of his felt hat in his hands, an unlikely gesture for a man so big and imposing. I had to smile to myself to see him that way over Sunbow, but my heart went out to him.

"Why don't we sit here in the kitchen," I said. "I'll bring us up a bottle of tomato wine."

Kelsey settled himself in the rocker, his hat still in hand. He seemed out of place indoors. I sat at the table, now and then replenishing our jelly glasses.

We talked about the weather at first, then Gabe Giles's cattle, their number and value, but I'm not one to waste good tomato wine on such topics, so I asked him to tell me about his life in the north country. As the wine was depleted, he warmed to his subject, stretched out his long legs and relaxed. He had a wealth of bear stories and gestures to go with them as grand as his voice. I could see why Sunbow loved him. We heard a cat's meow at the door and I let in Sugar-Tit, Sunbow's cat, a gray, long-haired beauty who recognized Kelsey at once and curled into his lap. He petted her as he talked.

It took three-quarters of the wine and a cushion of darkness for Kelsey to mention Sunbow. There had been a comfortable silence for a few minutes – comfortable for me, but now I see that he was mustering courage to ask me questions.

"Just where is this place in the woods?" he said. Sugar-Tit jumped from his lap like she knew a betrayal might be in the works. I got up and lit the lamp on the cedar chest.

"She asked me not to tell," I said. I fiddled with the wick, my back to Kelsey. He started rocking and the rocker crunched on the floorboards. Back at the table, I said, "Have some more, Kelsey. We might as well finish it off."

He held his tongue, though I could feel that he was mad. I gave him credit for that. Like a lot of big men, he knew how to keep his temper.

"How long have you known her?" he asked.

"Ten years," I said. "Ten years this spring."

"How did you come to be on this land?"

"It's mine," I said. "My father gave it to me."

"And the others?" Kelsey asked.

"Friends, just friends," I said.

Kelsey shook his head. His white hair seemed golden in the lamplight.

I decided to embellish just a bit. "Right now, of course, it's just the six of us on the land," I said. "Rachel lives in the tipi, Laremy doesn't come out of the woods often, and you've seen Crazy Heart around, haven't you? He lives in the dugout."

Kelsey nodded. "He's the one with the steam engine?"

"Right," I said. "And there's Little Egypt and Jade. Jade makes seven. But one summer we had fifty people here. That field below Little Egypt's place – the one that's gone to weeds – it was all planted in corn that year."

"We're so different," he said. It was as though he spoke to himself. I knew he meant himself and Sunbow, but in a large sense, he meant all of us. No getting around it, Kelsey had lived a different life.

He tipped his glass for the last time that night, picked up his hat, and made his good-byes, which were brief. He wasn't the kind of man to linger at the door for half an hour saying nothing. When he was gone I had a moment in bed to wonder what would happen, but sleep came fast and deep.

TWO DAYS LATER Sunbow returned. She looked a little peaked and I thought she had lost weight. Secretly, I thought that's why she did the fast each year – to keep her weight down. I had a barley-and-black-bean soup waiting for her and we had a good time that evening, talking in my kitchen over several pots of orange spice tea. She kept one ear cocked for the sound of Shasta's hooves or Kelsey's jeep. He didn't come, and finally around ten, she went back to her A-frame. I stood on the porch, watching the beam of her flashlight grow dim on the trail. This was the middle of July, but the wind was a cool wind. I spotted Cassiopeia in the northern sky.

I wasn't surprised that Kelsey didn't come right over. A man has his pride. I had the feeling he was mulling over the differences, whether he could stand them. We'd talked about it for months, so the next day Sunbow and I left for

Hawk Island to visit friends. We left the animals and garden in the care of our neighbors.

We drove my car, a 1963 Volkswagen. We drove by sawmills and through orchard country, where they were picking cherries. The hills were browning already from the heat. All the while Sunbow and I reminisced about times gone by and she never mentioned Kelsey once.

Hawk Island is in the middle of a lake. Three women, Harmony, Lillian, and Sue-Sue, live there. They once lived in the canyon with us until Sue-Sue inherited the Island from her grandmother, who had built a fishing lodge there in the forties – just a run-down cedar shake house surrounded by ponderosa pines. The three of them had a fantasy about living together and two years ago they moved from the canyon. We manage to keep in touch.

It was early evening when we arrived at the dirt parking strip where the raft was moored. Our clothes stuck to us from the heat and the cool air off the lake was welcome relief. We locked the car and secured our packs, sleeping bags, and a box of groceries – treats like cream cheese and avocados – to the raft. Sue-Sue, the handy one, had built the raft herself. It was six feet long, made of stout pine logs, and there were two splintery wooden gray paddles. They use a canoe to go back and forth and leave the raft for unexpected guests.

The lake was smooth, the trees along the shore reflected in clear lines. We paddled kneeling and within twenty minutes we were in sight of the house and Lillian, waving frantically from the front door. We paddled next to the rickety dock and tied the raft.

Lillian's white mongrel dog came wagging up to us, his

tail full of burrs. He had one bad eye, milky-blue, that rolled off to one side and gave him a maimed look. I never could see what she saw in him. But he was a good dog and never slobbered on me, so I could stand him. His name is Haiku.

I shouldered my pack and gathered a rolled sleeping bag in each arm. Lillian came down the path and tried to hug me, in spite of my load.

"You came to rescue me," she said. "The solitude is driving me crazy."

She hugged Sunbow, too. They had once been on the verge of becoming lovers and now it struck me that Sunbow wanted especially to see Lillian after being with Kelsey.

"Where is everyone?" Sunbow said.

"Picking cherries," Lillian said. She lifted the box of groceries. "They've been gone a week." Lillian is a teacher and it is her income which supports them primarily. Each morning all winter she goes to school in the nearby town. When summer comes, there is no orchard work for her. She stays home and keeps the chickens from scratching in the garden.

We followed her toward the house. Statuesque Leghorns strutted in the dirt near the split-rail fence. Lillian walked with a real swing to her stride, athletic in spite of a limpy ankle that had never quite healed. She had had a skiing accident years before. She was tall and tanned, wearing a ragged plaid smock over white painter's pants, cut off and rolled snug above her thighs. Summer was always good to Lillian.

The porch sprawled into the yard from all sides of the house, a welcoming. We set our loads down. It was a wide veranda, the floor boards worn smooth and gray. There were wooden chairs with bright, woven cushions and a chaise lounge with a yellow pillow in the shape of a sun like a child would draw, with floppy tubular rays. Plants hung in baskets from the ceiling.

"Just let me get us a drink," Lillian said. "We'll celebrate." She slammed through the screen door and Sunbow and I sat down. Over the door, someone had carved a motto: *Work, Love, Suffer.* From far away came the sound of a motor boat, probably from shore, anglers coming out for the evening catch.

"This is great," Sunbow said. "I needed this." She fanned herself with a magazine she had picked up from the floor.

It was not like Sunbow to be so still about Kelsey. Usually, when she was in love, she talked and talked, dissecting the experience, trying to understand, wanting to know all the possible angles. *What could happen. What he might have meant.* I tried to imagine Kelsey riding to Sunbow's house and discovering her absence. I felt a moment of empathy for him.

Lillian returned with three gin-and-tonics on a wicker tray. She bumped the screen door open with her hip. "Ice! We have ice now," she said. "Sue-Sue got her refrigerator working."

We relaxed into the cushions and the drinks. The chickens clucked around the porch and the dog sat there grinning like he was having a private joke on us all. A breeze whipped across the lake and cooled us. The mainland shore was just a curling green blur on the horizon.

"Now tell me what's new and exciting," Lillian said. I noticed a silvery streak in her short brown hair. She was thirty-seven. It always amazes me when I see that we are aging.

"I'm in love," Sunbow said. She and Lillian laughed together.

"He rides a white horse," I said.

"Wouldn't you know," Lillian said. "Now be serious. Tell me all about him."

There ensued a lengthy discussion of Kelsey. After a few minutes I slipped away for a walk.

The Island was a lush green place, not like the coastal islands, of course, but still more wet than our territory at the farm. A trail circumnavigated its perimeter, winding through the deep, razor-edged grasses, over gravel beaches, and within a grove of cottonwoods and pine. In the trees, pinemat covered the earth on either side of the path. Exposed weather-polished tree roots, like the bones of last season's deer, molded step-downs of packed dirt. I was on the Island but I could not be there completely. My mind always wandered back home, wondering about the animals, the garden. I sat down on a flat rock on the southern shore. A cormorant landed on a boulder out in the lake. Ground squirrels scurried among the rocks, inspecting me, waiting to see if I would leave any crumbs.

I sat there for a long time. I thought of Crazy Heart, the way it is with us. He is my neighbor and brother more than my husband. He cares for the animals when I'm gone. I share venison with him, he gives me a grouse now and then. We go for days on end without seeing one another, even though he lives in the dugout just across the road and down the lane a ways. Yet we lean on one another, on the presence of an old friend.

"No thinking," Sunbow said, startling me. She handed me a sweater.

"You should talk," I said. The light was growing golden, a summer dusk.

"Lilly's making a salad. We put the wine in the fridge to chill."

I put on the sweater and there were three sunflower seeds in one pocket. I left them there for the ground squirrels. We started walking, Sunbow in front since the path was wide enough for only one.

"Doesn't it surprise you that we're all getting older?" I said.

"Sort of," Sunbow said over her shoulder. "I think of us as young still."

"The gray hair and the personalities don't go together," I said.

"I'm old enough to be a grandmother," she said.

"A young grandmother."

We walked for awhile without talking until we came to a clearing of vetch and thistle where someone had piled clean new lumber.

"What's this?" I said.

"You won't believe it," Sunbow said. "Lilly has a friend, a man. He's building a little house here."

"A lover?" I said.

"What else?" Sunbow said. "She says this is it."

"Everybody's settling down."

"About time," she said. We kept walking, around the lumber and the dirt heaps.

Haiku barked a token bark as we approached the house. The windows were soft yellow squares of kerosene lamplight. Foxglove glowed along the side of the house.

On the porch, before we went in, I said, "Do you miss Kelsey?" There was a flash of heat lightning in the western sky.

"I miss him. Yeah," she said. "Do you think we have a chance?"

"I really don't know," I said. And we went inside for supper.

We stayed one more night. Though it was plain to see the attraction between Sunbow and Lillian, I don't think they did more than hold one another in a sisterly way. From their talk, it seemed they were each too much in love with the men to be in love with one another. I thought this was good. Sunbow didn't need to complicate her life.

We drove back to the farm, eager to can the cherries we picked in the orchards on the way home. We sped down the canyon, leaving a wake of dust, and who did we see but Kelsey, first thing, riding Shasta with Jade in the saddle with him. She was laughing and having a good time and Kelsey looked like he was, too.

We stopped the green Volkswagen beside him. He was on Sunbow's side.

"Hello Kelsey," Sunbow said.

"Hello Sunbow," he said. They were so formal, but they were glad to see one another, that was obvious – they were straining at the bit. They forgot me entirely.

"Stop by and visit on your way home," Sunbow said, by way of invitation.

"I might do that," Kelsey said.

They forgave one another. He spent the night. And after that it seemed things might work out between them. They returned to their habits, the early morning breakfast, Kelsey braiding her hair.

IN LOOKING BACK, I mark our trip to Hawk Island as the middle of the summer. After that, time flew. The garden came in and it was nothing but work, day into night. We had so many green beans we sold them at the co-op in the city. The zucchini were thick and we had a zucchini war one evening, slap-happy with the exhaustion of harvesting.

Our third cutting of alfalfa was a good one and we were blessed with sunshine as it lay in windrows. We waited until evening to pitch the hay onto the flatbed and take it to the barn.

Sunbow came by for me on her way to the alfalfa field. She wore a faded pair of gym shorts and work boots with gray socks stretched out around the ankles. Her braids were pinned against her head, out of the way. The sun crested the canyon wall as we walked to the field, our pitchforks over our shoulders. The heat had been heavy during the day. We were still warm enough to work without our shirts.

This was our practice: Little Egypt, with Jade beside her strapped into a car seat, drove Crazy Heart's truck, an old brown Dodge, with the flatbed hitched to the back bumper. One of us – this time it was Laremy who came out of the woods for the occasion – stood on the flatbed, accepting the forkloads of alfalfa the rest of us sent his way. Laremy liked the work and he received his share of milk for it.

The land grew tawny with evening as Crazy Heart, Sunbow, Rachel, and I loaded the flatbed, walking around and around the field. It was a big job for so few people and I remembered a time when the work went faster, when life was richer with personalities.

We worked for hours until the dark lay over us like a blue scarf. At the barn, someone brought a quart of home-brew.

We filled the barn, beginning to shiver in our sweat, itching with the hay, and the smell of the hay, the barn, the milky odor, warmed my heart. This was home. I was feeling all these generous thoughts, right with the world, when Kelsey appeared on Shasta.

Sunbow sat on a chopping block, legs out straight, her shirt open to the waist and vibrant, the way some women look after working hard. I was rolling a cigarette and the others were quiet, just settling into the good feeling after a job well done.

"You're going to catch your death of cold out here without your clothes," Kelsey said. His voice was hard as nails. It was plain what he meant.

Shasta looked blue in the darkness, like the snowberries dripping in the brush along the barbed-wire fence. He stomped his front hooves a bit and seemed tense, as tense as the rest of us. I removed a flake of tobacco from my tongue and then lit the cigarette, glad for something to do.

"It's summertime, Kelsey," Sunbow said. Her voice was a whisper, but it seemed she was shouting inside. Even as she spoke she pulled the work shirt together in front. I hated to see her feel ashamed.

"Come on," Kelsey said. "I'll ride you home."

"No thanks," Sunbow said.

"Have it your way," he said, and he reined Shasta around and went away.

"Damn right," Sunbow snapped. But Kelsey didn't hear her. She didn't intend for him to. Their disagreement cast a pall on our gathering and folks began to drift away after a few minutes until only Sunbow and I were left.

"Can I roll one?" she said.

I passed her the cloth bag and the rolling papers.

"What do you think of our chances now?" she said, squinting, sprinkling tobacco into the crease of the rolling paper.

"That depends on how much you're willing to change," I said. And we sat there smoking in the dark for awhile before we went our separate ways. I thought it was over.

Kelsey didn't come around and Sunbow began making plans to go apple-picking. Her birthday came and went near the end of September and we hardly mentioned it.

She went picking in October. In the orchards, she came down with a sickness. I was busy getting my wood in for the winter, spending each day alone with the saw and ax, seeking out dead fir to haul home. I hadn't even checked the mail for a few days. I didn't know she was sick until Kelsey brought her home in his jeep, two weeks to the day after she had left. She had called Gabe Giles and asked for Kelsey and said she needed him and he went to her. This seemed a most positive event if you can call a bacterial infection from drinking water a positive event. There was hope for them yet.

He nursed her back to health. We had our first hard frost and still Kelsey and Sunbow could not make up their minds. One day they would be seen laughing and sawing wood together, each on one end of a misery whip, under the bare tamaracks, and the next day she would come over with a tale of woe and he would be leaving for Woodpecker, a hard way to be heading into winter.

"There are some things I'm willing to change," Sunbow said, "and others I'm not." We were churning apples through the cider press, near Sunbow's wood shed. The juice from the apple pulp trickled down our sleeves and we were a mess, our hands and cheeks chapped, but proud of the twenty quarts we had pressed so far.

"Like what?" I said.

"Like I'd learn to clean his birds. He thinks it's ridiculous that I've never learned to clean chickens and birds. Fish. I *can* clean fish," she said. I heard a chainsaw in the distance.

"What else?" I said.

"What else?" she said.

"What else are you willing to change?"

"Look at the geese," Sunbow said, pointing at the honking wedge above the southern rimrock. "I don't know if he really wants to go back north," she said. "My turn. You toss the apples." She took over for me at the wheel.

The next morning was overcast. About noon, Kelsey drove to my place in his jeep. He was dressed in a sheepskin coat, a hat that covered his ears, and mittens. His jeep was packed tight with duffel bags, saddle bags, and suitcases. It was hard for me to imagine him carrying a suitcase.

I asked him to lunch.

We drank some Earl Grey tea and waited for the leftovers – venison chili – to warm on the cookstove.

"I'm leaving, Virginia. I quit Gabe today," he said.

"Have a little honey in your tea," I said. "Where you headed?"

"Back to where I came from," he said. I didn't press him further for the details. I'd heard it all from her.

We had a cozy lunch and, as luck would have it, the snow began falling as we sat there afterwards. He polished off his milk, scraped his chair back, and wiped his mouth on the checkered napkin.

"I've got to be going," he said. "I'll stop and say good-bye to her, too."

"I should think so," I thought, but aloud I said, "All the best to you, Kelsey." And we shook hands.

I watched from the kitchen window as he drove down the lane that runs from my house to Sunbow's. I saw her come out on the porch and I saw him go in. After that the snow really flew. An hour later, after I had cleaned up the kitchen and written a letter to the Hawk Island people, I looked out the window and his jeep was still there, blurred in the curtain of snow. And there it remained all winter.

Biographical Note

Patricia Henley was raised in Indiana and Maryland, and attended St. Mary's College and Johns Hopkins University, which awarded her an M.A. in writing in 1974. For three years, she lived at Tolstoy Farm, an anarchist, back-to-the-land community in Washington State. She is the author of a poetry chapbook, *Learning to Die*, published in 1979. In spring, 1984, she moved from British Columbia to Bozeman, Montana, and after a four-year hiatus from writing resumed writing fiction. She lives in Bozeman and works as a counselor at Women in Transition, a center for displaced homemakers.

89 076